THE VISION RETURNED THE FOLLOWING NIGHT, and every night thereafter, always exactly the same: a handsome boy of eighteen or twenty, dressed in fine clothes, holding a beautiful goblet.

Molly gazed thoughtfully at the play of water in the pond, thinking not about the cup but the boy who held it—it was like looking into a mirror. He was *herself*, had she been older and a boy.

It had to mean something—that uncanny resemblance, the nightly insistence of the vision. Wouldn't it be wonderful if, just this once, it portended something good?

Best not to count on it, though.

The
Cup and the Crown

Diane Stanley

HARPER
An Imprint of HarperCollinsPublishers

Library of Congress Cataloging-in-Publication Data
Stanley, Diane.
        The cup and the crown / Diane Stanley. — 1st ed.
            p.   cm.
        Summary: Sequel to: The silver bowl.
        Summary: "At King Alaric's urging, Molly sets off on a quest for a magi-
cal loving cup (a goblet that binds people together), and her journey leads
her to the hidden city of her ancestors, which proves to be as dangerous as it
is mysterious"— Provided by publisher.
        ISBN 978-0-06-196323-0 (pbk.)
        [1. Drinking cups—Fiction. 2. Identity—Fiction. 3. Clairvoyance—
Fiction. 4. Magic—Fiction. 5. Kings, queens, rulers, etc.—Fiction. 6.
Fantasy.] I. Title.
PZ7.S7869Cup   2012   2012025280
[Fic]—dc23   CIP
                                                                    AC

Typography by Adam B. Bohannon
13 14 15 16 17   CG/OPM   10 9 8 7 6 5 4 3 2 1
❖
First paperback edition, 2013

This book is dedicated to Peter,
who is always there to listen
and who says wonderful things, like,
What if you had a ratcatcher?

CONTENTS

The Cup
and the Crown

1

King Alaric the Younger

THE GREAT HALL WAS MUCH as she remembered it: the tapestries, the massive iron candle stands, the enormous fireplace, the great gilt screen behind the dais. But the rushes were gone from the floor now, in keeping with the latest fashion. And there were sentries posted at the entrance to the royal chambers. They followed her with their eyes as she paced in restless circles, waiting. What was taking Alaric so long?

There had never been guards in the old days, when Godfrey the Lame was king. Molly knew this for a fact. She'd once pressed her ear to that very door and listened to young Prince Alaric quarreling with his mother, unobserved by anyone but Tobias, who'd come to mend the fire. He'd been scandalized that a scullery maid should presume to eavesdrop on a queen.

Molly smiled, remembering how intensely she'd despised them both. "Mind who you look at, wench," Prince Alaric had said to her as he stormed out of his mother's room. And "You aren't fit to be here," Tobias had added later. What *she'd* said didn't bear repeating— but then she'd only been seven at the time, and inclined to say whatever popped into her head, however outrageous it might be.

Come to think of it, that last part hadn't changed so very much.

She circled past the dais and was musing on the screen when the door flew open and a large, imposing man came out, thunder on his face, his boots striking the flagstones with the force of his anger. As he passed, he shot Molly a look of pure revulsion. Then he turned away, as from something loathsome, and continued with long strides down the length of that cavernous room, the stink of his fury trailing behind. She watched him, appalled, till he was long out of sight. Only when she heard her name did she look back at the door and see Alaric standing there.

He didn't greet her with a smile or apologize for making her wait. Indeed, he scarcely looked at her at all.

"Come," he said. "We'll walk in the garden. I need a change of air."

He took her arm and held it close to his side. Whether he did this out of affection or was merely stiff with rage, Molly couldn't tell. Either way, she liked it. She cast a quick glance up at his pale, narrow face, his sun-bright curls and gray eyes, and judged him as handsome as ever—despite the scowl and the crease between his brows. She sighed to herself in quiet satisfaction and leaned her head against his shoulder, just a touch.

It was high summer, and the flower beds were bright with lilacs, roses, and lilies. Ancient trees arched over their heads, offering welcome shade as they followed their winding course, fine gravel crunching beneath their feet.

Molly had never been there before, though she'd lived half her life at Dethemere Castle. Common servants had no business in the king's garden, unless it was to plant, and prune, and tend that private little patch of paradise. Her place had been in the kitchen, scrubbing pots and polishing silver.

All that had changed this past half year. And nothing about her transformation from scullion to lady had struck her quite so forcibly as this: that she walked the paths of the royal garden on the arm of the king of Westria—just the two of them, alone.

Never mind that he was in a mood.

"So, how do you like your new estate?" He said this distractedly, his mind on something else.

"It's very beautiful, my lord."

"I should certainly hope so. It was to have been my sister's dower house. You're happy there?"

"Not especially, my lord."

He stopped and looked down at her, *really* looked for the first time that morning.

"'*Not especially*, my lord'?"

"It's too grand for me, Alaric. I don't belong. And those highborn servants, brought in to attend a princess, being asked to serve the likes of me . . ."

"You're a lady now, by royal decree."

"Yes. And you could royally decree that henceforth eels shall fly and magpies shall swim in the sea. But even *you* have not the power to make it so. My ladies of the chamber certainly know what I am. They correct my manners at table and express amazement that I can't do embroidery, or play the lute, or dance, or read romances. And there's nothing for me to do all day but meet with my steward and my chamberlain to talk about things I don't understand, and choose which gown to wear, and sit staring into the fire or out the window while my ladies drive me mad with their never-ending chatter."

"Merciful heavens! You're *bored* as well?"

"Unbearably."

She could feel the tension in his body. He held her arm in a viselike grip.

"Any minute now you're going to say that you're awfully sorry, you know you've been shockingly rude, but it's all because you were ill raised."

"I suppose that would be—"

"Well, *a plague* on your upbringing! I'm sick of hearing about it. I can see you now in your dotage." He took the high, nasal voice of an old crone, hunching his back for added effect. "Oh, I'm *so* sorry I insulted you, my lord, but when I was a small child—*fifty years* ago—I was not taught how to behave."

She took a deep breath. "Your Majesty," she said, "I truly *am* sorry that I seem so ungrateful when you have been so generous and kind. But I spoke the truth: I don't have the makings of a lady. You'd have done better to set me up as a shopkeeper—"

"If you say another word, I shall bite off your head."

How was it, she wondered as they continued to walk in stormy silence, that she'd been so careful of what she said to the cook when she'd worked in the palace kitchens and cowered under the haughty gazes of her ladies of the chamber—yet with the *king of Westria,* well, she'd say just *any* old thing!

"I'll find you some better attendants," he muttered, "and see that they treat you with respect."

When she didn't respond, he added, "You may speak now."

"Thank you, my lord, but you can leave them as they are. In the end I found it rather amusing to torture them."

"*Torture* them? Good God!"

"Not with thumbscrews, never fear. I just developed a sudden fondness for exercise—taking long walks to the village or the next town over, in foul weather whenever possible. And as I cannot go out alone, it being unfitting for a lady—"

"—they have to accompany you."

"Yes. Such a lot of mud this year."

She'd finally made him laugh. And it felt for a brief spell like the old times, before he'd become king and the burden of great responsibility had been laid on his young shoulders, along with his royal robes.

"Alaric," she said softly. "Tell me why I'm here." She already knew, of course. She'd known for weeks, long before the royal messenger had arrived at Barcliffe Manor, calling her back to court. She knew because she'd seen it in a vision.

The first time it had happened, she'd taken it for a dream. But it had been too clear, too perfect; and when she'd sat up in bed, it had stayed with her, not fading away like smoke into air as dreams always do. It had returned the following night, and every night thereafter, always exactly the same: a handsome boy of eighteen or twenty, dressed in fine clothes, holding a beautiful goblet. And though she'd never seen the cup before, she knew exactly what it was—and what it meant for her, and for the king.

As for the boy, he was a mystery.

"I want you to go to Austlind," Alaric said, "to find one of your grandfather's Loving Cups."

"I thought that must be it," she said. "You were so keen to have one last winter—then not another word. I kept expecting . . . but I suppose you've had a lot on your mind these past months."

"Learning to be a king, you mean? And taking control of my country, and choosing my counselors, and fending off officious busybodies who say I'm too young to rule and I must have a regent do it for me?"

"Yes. And I suppose that terrible man who came out of your chambers just now is one of the busybodies?"

"Lord Mayhew? Oh, yes. You know what he calls

me behind my back? King Alaric the Younger. Isn't that charming?"

"You should chop off his head."

"Oh, please, Molly, be serious. I'm sending him with you to Austlind, by the way, to see to your safety on the road. That's why he was so angry. He feels the mission is beneath him."

"Then why send him? If he mocks you in secret, surely he cannot be trusted."

"I trust him to keep you safe. As for the rest, I just told him you're going to Austlind to find a certain silver cup, which I want to send as a gift to the king of Cortova. Anything regarding the princess or the special properties of the cup—please keep that to yourself."

They'd reached an opening in the boxwood hedge that led to the heart of the garden. Here was a pond with a stone fish rising out of the center, standing upright on its tail, water spouting from its mouth.

They sat on a long stone bench in the shade of a chestnut tree. The king released her arm.

"Now, in addition to Lord Mayhew, I'm sending my valet. His name is Stephen, he's fluent in the language of Austlind, and he has my complete trust. You may speak freely with him in all things. But do it in private."

She nodded.

"You'll need a chaperone, of course. Winifred will do, if you wish."

"Yes. And I want Tobias, too."

He scowled. "Whatever for?"

"Have you some personal objection to Tobias?"

His hands flew up, impatient. "Fine," he said. "By all means, bring Tobias."

She waited a spell for his ruffled feathers to settle before making them rise again.

"Alaric?" she began carefully. "May I ask you a question?"

"I suppose that depends on what it is."

"I know you feel you must marry soon and get yourself an heir, as there is no one left in your family to inherit. What I don't understand is why you must resort to enchantment in order to get yourself a bride. I would think there'd be princesses waiting in line—"

He gripped his head with both hands as if fearing it might come off. "By all the saints in heaven, Molly— is there nothing you will not ask? God's blood, but your impertinence takes my breath away!"

She flushed. "I see I overstepped." And then, because she couldn't help it, "I thought I was your friend."

"Don't," he said, getting up from the bench and going to stand by the pond. He stayed there, not speaking, for an age and more. Then he came back and sat down beside her again.

"It will not be an easy match to make," he said. "When Princess Elizabetta was betrothed to my brother Edmund and came to Dethemere Castle in advance of the marriage, she was in the great hall that night, at my brother's side—"

"I know all that, Alaric. For heaven's sake, I was there."

"Then you will understand that after witnessing the slaughter of my family, including my poor brother whom she was meant to marry—and at such close hand that she was spattered with his very blood—the princess will not look warmly on a match with another king of Westria."

"I agree. It's hopeless. So why not just choose someone else?"

"Because it must be her."

"Oh, come now! She stole your heart in a single day? I know she's beautiful; I saw her myself. But you can't have exchanged a dozen words with the lady. How do you know she's not a shrew, or stupid, or wicked?"

"Neither my heart nor her beauty has anything to do with it, Molly. The kingdom of Cortova controls the Southern Sea. I can't afford to have them turn away from us and make an alliance elsewhere. And there's been talk of a match with Prince Rupert, my cousin Reynard's eldest son."

"That little runt? He can't be more than thirteen!"

"He's fourteen, just two years younger than I; and where royal marriages are concerned, age doesn't matter. If Rupert is matched with Elizabetta, it'll be a disaster for us. Austlind is already allied to Erbano through Reynard's marriage to Beatrice. If they combine with Cortova too, they'll be so powerful, I fear we could not stand against them.

"So I must have an alliance with Cortova. To achieve that, I must wed the princess. And to wed the princess I must, as you so graciously put it, resort to enchantment. Is that clear?"

"As a mountain stream, my lord."

"Good. Now, you'll be going to a crafts town called Faers-Wigan, where your grandfather worked his trade. If one of his cups is still to be had, you should find it there. But I'm a little concerned—"

"—that I won't be able to tell a true cup from a false one?"

He nodded. "There are a lot of dishonest traders who'll be eager to make a sale, and they'll claim—"

"I know. But they won't fool me. I've been seeing the cup in my dreams this past month and more. I could describe it to you down to the finest detail."

The king brightened upon hearing this. He trusted her magical gift, innocent of the dreadful price she'd paid for the knowledge it brought her. He didn't know—because she'd never told him—how profoundly she dreaded those visions, which came to her unbidden, forcing her to look on unspeakable things. And he certainly couldn't imagine that brash, bold, tough little Molly was haunted by the murder of her grandfather, which she'd witnessed in one of those visions, and the terrible fate of her gentle mother, locked up as a madwoman in a small, dim, noisome room till she was released by death—all because they shared the same magical gift that Molly now carried.

She gazed thoughtfully at the play of water in the pond, thinking not about the cup but the boy who held it: that face, with its straight nose and fine chin, those clear gray eyes, that dark, curly hair—it was like looking into a mirror. He was *herself*, had she been older and a boy.

It had to mean something—that uncanny resemblance, the nightly insistence of the vision. Wouldn't it be wonderful if, just this once, it portended something good?

Best not to count on it, though.

⚜ 2 ⚜

A Lonely Road

THE WEATHER WAS PERFECT for a journey: the cloudless sky a brilliant blue, the warm air sweet with the smell of clover, the road shaded by ancient plane trees, which rustled in the breeze. And overhead, a pair of ravens danced together—swooping in tandem, dipping and rising, floating on currents of air. It was as if they were joined by invisible strings.

"Look at that!" Molly said, craning her neck to watch. "See how they stay together so perfectly."

"They're courting," Stephen said. "Ravens pair for life, you know."

"Oh, I wish I could do that, just once!"

"Go a-courting?" asked Winifred with a wicked smile.

"*No*, you goose! Fly! I want to rise up into the clouds and float on the air."

"Wouldn't we all?" Stephen said.

They continued in silence, watching in fascination, listening to the birdsong in the meadows and trees and the soft plodding of the horses—all but Tobias, who stared down the road deep in thought.

When he and Molly had first met, he'd been the kitchen's donkey boy, an unkempt, scruffy, troubled child of nine who'd just lost his family to the plague. She'd been the lowest of the scullions, an unkempt, scruffy, impetuous, mannerless child of seven who'd lost her mother to madness and her father to drink and disinterest. She'd told Tobias to wipe his nose and shut his mouth so people wouldn't take him for a half-wit; he'd said she didn't deserve to work at Dethemere Castle and probably wouldn't last there a week.

They'd been inseparable ever since.

When, exactly, things had started to change, Tobias couldn't quite remember. It came to him at odd moments, this sense that she was something more than a friend. There were times when he was gripped with a terrible foreboding that he might lose her some-day, as he'd lost his family; and he knew he could not survive it. From this he understood that she'd become essential to his life.

There was a word for that, but he'd never spoken it. He was afraid to, and rightly so. That wasn't how they related to each other. The most affectionate thing she'd ever said was "Don't you die on me, Tobias! I couldn't bear it."

He'd wondered many a time whether she felt the same things he did but kept it close to her chest as was her nature. She hadn't grown up with affection. It must seem strange to her. But was the thought of courting really such an outrage that she'd call Winifred a goose for even suggesting it?

"And what are *you* so glum about, prune-face?" Molly said. "On this beautiful day, when ravens are courting and we're off on an adventure?"

"Nothing at all," he said.

Just then a breeze kicked up and caught the brim of Molly's hat—a disreputable-looking thing she'd bought from one of the gardeners—and sent it flying. Tobias, ever quick, caught it in midair and returned it to Molly with a bow from the waist. She smiled at him like an angel, then crammed it gracelessly back on her head.

And suddenly his dejection vanished. *Of course* she loved him, in her own strange way, and that was more than enough. Indeed, he wondered, in a surge of emotion, if one day, looking back on his life as an old man, he'd choose this moment to have been the happiest of all, the time when he felt the most hopeful and at peace with the world.

*   *

As the days passed, the landscape began to change. The air grew cooler and pines began to replace the plane trees, the chestnuts, and the oaks. In the distance were great, rugged mountains, half shrouded in mist. And then, shortly before sunrise on their sixth day, they crossed the border into Austlind.

Only then did Mayhew announce the change of plans.

They would not be taking the common route that skirted the mountains, winding through the southern foothills before turning north again. Instead, they'd cut directly across the range through a narrow mountain pass. The road was rarely used, being steep and in poor repair; but if they rode hard before the climbing began, they might reach Faers-Wigan by nightfall.

This was contrary to Alaric's explicit instructions. And considering all the precautions they'd taken against being robbed—dressing as common folk, hiding the king's gold in many secret compartments—it seemed odd to choose the very sort of lonely road where thieves were most likely to be lurking. But no one dared argue with Mayhew, not even Molly.

The short route it would be, then.

Around midmorning they left the broad highway, crossed the river, and continued north and east on a narrow horse path. Trees, tall grass, and scrub grew thickly on both sides, encroaching on the roadway. Here and there potholes, fit to break a horse's leg, were hidden by the undergrowth. Mayhew reined in his horse and they proceeded at a walk.

Above them a raven circled, riding the warm updraft of air. "He's following us," Tobias said.

"*Leading* us, more like," said Winifred. "He flies straight along the path till he gets too far ahead, then he circles back over us, like now."

Stephen laughed. "The countryside is full of ravens, and they all look exactly the same."

"No," Molly said. "Winifred's right. I've been watching him too, and it's the same bird, no question."

Stephen shrugged. "Whatever you say."

"Our raven guide," Molly muttered to herself, pleased with the image.

Before long the path began to rise. In places it was too narrow even for two to ride abreast, so they formed a single file and continued at a walk so as not to overtax the horses on the steep incline.

Mayhew looked back to see how it had fallen out. Molly was close behind him, followed by Tobias, then Winifred, with Stephen taking the rear. He would rather have had Tobias in back—for though the boy had no apparent skill with a sword, he was tall, strong, and probably quick, while Stephen was none of those things. But it would take time to stop and rearrange the order, so he let it go.

That was a mistake. And he compounded it by failing to notice how much stronger his mount was than the others. It might not look like a warhorse, but that's what it was. And so, as the way twisted and turned through the steep and rocky terrain, the space between them grew, particularly a gap between Tobias and Winifred, who'd stopped to pull out her cloak.

❧ ❦

The thief had been hiding in the wilderness since escaping from prison, living off the land and waiting for someone to pass on that godforsaken road. Now the moment had arrived, bringing with it the chance to get both money and a horse. He might lose his life in the attempt, but that would be better than dying of starvation in the woods.

The girl would be easy. The only problem was the man behind her. He was armed, though the sword was probably just for show. There was a softness about him that was telling; he wouldn't put up much of a fight.

The man in the lead, though, he was a knight for sure. The thief would have to work fast before he could ride back to the rescue. But it was doable: he'd just have to take the little fellow by surprise, knock him off his horse, grab his purse, then leap into the saddle and ride like the devil. By the time the girl had finished screaming and the knight had made his way back—working his way around the girl and the boy in the middle—the thief would have disappeared.

He knew the woods now, and the hiding places.

Winifred was just fastening her cloak—Stephen watching uneasily, aware of the growing space between her and Tobias—when the raven came swooping down and gave a loud, anxious cry. It was a warning, Stephen was sure of it; but when he looked around, he saw nothing.

That was because the thief had come in from behind and was hiding under the horse's rump. Now, still crouching down, he reached up and grabbed the hem of Stephen's cloak. Yanking hard, he pulled him out of the saddle. But Stephen's left foot caught in the stirrup, and the terrified horse danced away to the right, trying to free itself of this unnatural burden. Winifred screamed.

The thief decided to leave the man dangling where

he was and take the girl's horse instead. But she proved more quick-witted than expected. She gave her mount a vicious kick and darted out of his reach, crying "Help, help!" and nearly colliding with the tall boy who'd already turned back.

There was still a chance to get what he wanted if he acted fast. He easily cut the purse from his victim's belt; now all he had to do was get the boot out of the stirrup. But it wouldn't come; the weight of the man's inert body was holding it in place. The thief had just decided to cut his losses and run—at least he had the purse, and with all the trees and underbrush, they couldn't follow him on horseback—when the tall boy came thundering in and leaped out of the saddle, dagger at the ready.

It wasn't even a contest. By the time Mayhew arrived and made a more practiced leap from his mount, Tobias had the man pinned to the ground, the knife at his throat.

"Move," Mayhew said, pulling Tobias roughly away by the collar and dispatching the thief with a single slash of his sword. Then, once he'd satisfied himself that Stephen was all right, he grabbed hold of the dead man's feet and started dragging the body away.

"What are you doing?" Tobias asked.

"What does it look like?"

As there was no obvious response to that question, Tobias didn't give one; but it was plain that Mayhew wasn't simply clearing the road. He was hauling the corpse into the forest.

"But we can't just leave him there," Molly said when Mayhew returned alone. "Shouldn't we give the hue and cry?"

He stared at her, incredulous.

"That's the law," Tobias said.

"All right. And who, pray tell, will hear our hue and cry? That blasted raven there? Perhaps we should turn back and ride to the nearest town—we might get there by nightfall—and see if they want to send a coroner up here to determine the cause of death, then carry the body back down the mountain so they can dump it into a pauper's grave."

"I see your point," Molly said.

❧ 3 ❧

Faers-Wigan

THE GOLDSMITHS' GUILD had the largest and grandest trade hall in Faers-Wigan. It looked more like a palace than a business establishment, with floors of marble, walls hung with tapestries, and torch stands plated with gold. The building served as a gathering place for the members of the guild—goldsmiths and silversmiths alike—and held offices for its many officials.

The guildhall also had a library where the archives were kept, an airy, pleasant room with bookshelves running along the walls. In the center was a large oak table, at the far end of which sat the guild's librarian, whose name was Joseph.

Light streamed in through tall windows onto the dome of his balding head. He was old and pale, as though the sun had bleached him out, and what little hair he had was fine and fair. But his eyes were bright, and so were his wits. Not only could he find the information they were seeking, he could do it in their own language.

He went to a shelf, quickly found the correct volume, and brought it back to the table. Then he started turning pages, leaning forward now and again to squint at an entry, shaking his head and turning to the next one. At last he seemed to have found something, but he didn't say a word; he just opened a little box and took out a thin stick of yellow wood. This he carefully laid between the pages to act as a bookmark, then continued with his search.

Molly sat quietly, watching him and waiting. After a while she noticed that Stephen was looking down at the table, or gazing idly around the room—not staring unendingly at Joseph as she was doing. *Of course,* she thought; he was being polite. No one likes to be stared at. So she looked down at her hands, noticed a smudge, and was just wetting her fingers in her mouth to wipe the smudge away when she heard a gravelly snort. She turned to see Winifred, her head lolling forward, her mouth agape, and her eyes closed. Oh, they were such a hopeless pair of bumpkins! She nudged her friend with an elbow, then discreetly wiped her fingers on her skirt.

Joseph still studied the book in silence, flipping pages, stopping, reading, moving on. Now and then a look of triumph would cross his face and he'd tuck in a strip of wood to mark a page. At last it seemed he was done. He turned back to the beginning, folded his hands on the tabletop, and spoke.

"The first mention of your grandfather, William Harrows, is in May of 1358," he said. "It's in regard to a contract of employment in the workshop of Artur Volkmann. At the same time William was entered into our rolls as a journeyman silversmith, though there's no record of his apprenticeship and no mention of who his master might have been. We must therefore assume that he came here from somewhere else. Harrows is probably a place-name, his town of origin."

"Oh," Molly said, disappointed. "I'd hoped to find some relatives here."

"That's very unlikely," he said, tapping a bony finger thoughtfully on a corner of the book. "Wherever he came from, William should have had a document of release showing that he'd completed his term of service. But the records just say that he'd proved his competence to Master Volkmann's satisfaction. Quite frankly, I find that suspicious."

Molly's hackles went up. "What do you mean, 'suspicious'?"

"It suggests that your grandfather may have broken his contract and run away. In a case like that, who can tell what other crimes he might also have committed—thievery, for example, or worse—that forced him to leave his master, and indeed his native country? Of course, it's also possible that he was set loose by some tragedy or other: plague, or fire, or accident. "

He stared into the distance for a moment, eyes half closed, quite unaware that Molly was red-faced and scowling.

"There's something else that strikes me as odd," he said, lifting his brows in emphasis. "William Harrows was only seventeen at the time. His apprenticeship would have taken seven years. He would have to have started at ten, which is . . . unusual."

"Perhaps the rules were different in his home country," Stephen suggested.

"Perhaps." Joseph turned to the next marked section. "This should please you, my lady," he said. "Remarkable—truly remarkable! At the age of twenty-two your grandfather submitted a masterpiece to the guild. That was very bold of him, being so young and new to the town. He cannot have imagined he'd be accepted. But he applied all the same. The work is described as"—he leaned forward and read, following the text with his finger—"'a silver-gilt cup with a lid decorated with pearls set in filigree and embellished with transparent enamels of astonishing quality.' Master Volkmann testified under oath that the work was wholly William's own and he had not assisted him in any way.

"The piece must have been extraordinary for it to have been accepted," he went on. "The old men on the committee would have been hard set against it: *'This will set a dangerous precedent! He must wait his turn!'* And yet it *was* accepted, and William Harrows became the youngest master in the history of our guild."

"Oh!" Molly said. "That does please me, very much."

"I thought it would. Now, right below that is a second entry. Artur Volkmann and William Harrows entered into a partnership that same day—which is, again, highly unusual. Buying half a share of a large, established business would be beyond the means of a young man on a journeyman's salary."

"Are you suggesting—?"

"It's just curious, that's all—or at least it was till I read the next entry. On August 12, 1366, William married his new partner's daughter, Martha."

"That means Artur Volkmann was—"

"Your great-grandfather. Yes." He turned to the next page.

"This one is dated February 3, 1368: 'Master Artur Volkmann departed this life at the age of fifty-three. He was accompanied to the churchyard by his family and the members of the guild, etcetera, etcetera. . . . His last will and testament was established by probate, etcetera, etcetera . . . the beneficiary being his partner, William Harrows.'" He looked up at Molly. "That made him a very wealthy man. Quite a feat for a boy who arrived here . . . well . . ."

Molly heaved a loud sigh of disgust. Joseph didn't seem to notice.

"'On December tenth of that same year, a daughter was born to William Harrows, master goldsmith, and his wife, Martha.' No name is given."

"It was Greta," Molly said.

He nodded and turned to the final entry but paused for a moment before reading it. "'November 23, 1369, Master William Harrows was found dead in his workshop. In the absence of any family, the funeral was arranged by the guild.'"

He folded his hands on the table again. "That's everything in the records. But it was common knowledge at the time that William was murdered."

"I know."

"Indeed?" He looked at her pointedly. "Well, since the wife and child were nowhere to be found, it was assumed that they had been taken, and most likely killed, by whoever had done the murder. Yet now here you are, saying you are William's granddaughter. So I gather that the child at least—"

"Greta."

"You claim that she survived."

"Yes, I *do* claim it, for it is true. My grandmother fled to Westria with the baby and settled there."

"Ah. I suppose you've come for the inheritance, then."

"No!" she said, rising to her feet. "I have *not* come for his money. I came to learn my grandfather's history."

"All the same," Joseph said, rising as well out of politeness, "I should tell you that William's fortune was seized by the crown, there being no surviving heirs. So if you change your mind and decide to pursue it, you'll have to prove that you are indeed William's grandchild. And even then—"

"I will *not* pursue it."

"As you wish. Is there anything else you need?"

"No," said Molly.

"Yes," said Stephen at exactly the same time. "The address of William's shop."

⟨ 4 ⟩

The Workshop of
William Harrows

THEY LEFT THE GUILDHALL and headed for the commercial district, Stephen leading the way. He took Molly's arm and leaned over to speak softly into her ear. "The man didn't mean to offend you," he said.

"Really? He all but said my grandfather slit his master's throat, then robbed him and ran away."

"Excuse me, my lady, but you exaggerate."

"I didn't like him."

"Well, he was useful, was he not?"

"I suppose."

They turned down Silk Row and continued at an unhurried pace, admiring the goods on display: furs, lace, velvets, brocades, cloth-of-gold, and silken veils as fine as spiderwebs. Apprentices waiting outside shop doors perked up as they approached. "Something for the ladies?" they'd ask. "Won't you come in and have a look?"

But Stephen would just nod and smile. "Not today, thank you," he'd say.

At last they came to Goldsmith's Lane, where he paused, looking thoughtfully up and down the street, wondering from which end the blocks were numbered.

"I think they start from the center of town," Mayhew said.

"Yes. You're right. In that case we should turn to the left."

Winifred stopped to stare at a window display of brooches, belt fittings, signets, and sword hilts, all made from silver or gold, engraved or worked with fine enamels, inlaid with ivory, or set with precious jewels. "Oh!" she moaned. "Will you look at that?"

Instantly the apprentices were upon them.

"Just looking," Stephen said, gently taking Winifred's arm and urging her forward. "It's best to keep moving," he whispered.

They continued in the same leisurely manner, trying not to stare, until Stephen stopped before a particularly handsome doorway framed by a stone arch, its double doors open wide. Above the entrance was a painted wooden sign. The image was simple: the silhouette of a goblet rendered in silver on a field of blue. Molly recognized the shape at once. It was the Loving Cup, exactly as she'd seen in her dreams.

And perched on the post that held the sign was her raven.

"This is the place," she said.

⇒ ⇐

The sound of hammering filled the workshop—*tink, tink, tink*—as busy hands worked to form the shape of bowls or cups against the curved necks of little anvils. One man was pressing designs into a silver tray, carefully placing his punch, then striking it smartly with a hammer: *thunk!* Over by the forge, a journeyman and an apprentice did double-duty with the bellows.

Molly closed her eyes and tried to recall her grandfather's workshop as she'd seen it in her visions. There'd been shelves to display his fine silver pieces against the right-hand wall, and the central worktable had been smaller. But the forge was in the same place, and she remembered the graceful arched window that filled the end wall of the long, narrow room. Yes, she was sure. This had once been the workshop of William Harrows, the place where Molly had watched him die.

"My lady?" Stephen said, gently touching her arm. "Will you please step this way?"

He guided her back toward the front of the room where a stocky man waited, looking very grand in saffron-colored silk. Pinned to his wine-red velvet cap was a handsome brooch: four pearls set in a diamond shape with a single ruby drop hanging from its lowest point.

"Lady Marguerite," Stephen said in his best courtly manner, "may I present Master Frears, the owner of this shop."

The man bowed and his ruby danced.

"Master Frears purchased this shop from another goldsmith, who had bought it years before from the crown. But he's certainly heard of William Harrows, who is something of a legend in Goldsmith's Lane, and assures me that this used to be his workshop."

"Did you ask about the Loving Cups?" she said in Westrian.

"Not yet. I'll do it now."

While Stephen asked the question in flawless Austlinder, Molly scanned the countertops and shelves. There were any number of goblets on display, but all of them were in the new style, slender and tall. So unless Master Frears had some old pieces locked away somewhere . . .

Suddenly she realized how unlikely that was. The workshop and all of its contents had been seized by the crown. Besides the building, that would have included the tools and furnishings; William's stock of silver and gold, jewels, ivory, pearls, coral, and onyx; and any finished pieces that had not been sold. It would have been the same with the family's home. The king's men would have come and carried everything away, from Greta's cradle and Martha's gowns to the pots and andirons in the kitchen. If there'd been a Loving Cup in either place, King Reynard had it now.

Disheartened, she turned back to Master Frears just as Stephen was rounding off his question. She saw the goldsmith cast a quick glance around the room, trying to decide which of several goblets he could pass off as a Loving Cup.

Was it even worth the effort of going through the motions, looking at what he had to offer, shaking her head, watching as he grew ever more desperate and offered her still more expensive cups her grandfather hadn't made? Yet they'd come so far to find the cup. And what if Master Frears should suddenly remember: "Oh, you must mean *that* old thing—excuse me, I meant that *classically beautiful* piece up there on the top shelf hidden behind the silver-gilt bowl?"

It wasn't likely, but it *might* happen.

She was staring at the floor, trying to decide what to do, when she had the distinct impression that she was being watched.

I see you! said a voice in her head.

Molly looked up and saw a stooped old man sitting in a corner at the back of the shop. He was polishing a small bowl with a white cloth and gazing fixedly in her direction. She tugged gently at Stephen's sleeve to get his attention. "There are no Loving Cups in this shop," she whispered, "but keep him busy, will you? There's something I need to find out."

Stephen nodded and returned to the goldsmith while Molly wandered away.

The old man's face didn't change as she came closer. He just continued to stare straight ahead. And then she understood. He hadn't been looking at her at all—the man was stone-blind.

Yet he spoke to her again in that strange way. His lips weren't moving and she wasn't hearing a voice, yet she knew exactly what he was saying.

You're one of them, ain't you?

She squatted down so they were face to face. "What did you mean, 'You're *one of them*'? One of who?"

He rocked back and forth on his stool.

One of them magical folk from Harrowsgode.

"No. I've never heard of Harrowsgode. But my grandfather was called William Harrows, and he wasn't born here; he came from somewhere else. Is that the place, then? Harrowsgode?"

Aye. He was magical, too. He's dead now.

She caught her breath, trying to stay calm. "Did you know him—William Harrows?"

I was his shop boy, till he were murdered. I saw him lyin' right there. He pointed to a spot by the forge. *Right there he was. Strangled.*

Molly shivered, picturing this man, just a young boy then, coming in to sweep up the shop and finding his master's body. No, she suddenly realized—more likely he was there all along. He watched the murder through a keyhole. Then when it was safe, he came creeping out and rifled through her grandfather's pockets, looking for coins. Or slipped the rings off his fingers.

He didn't need it anymore.

She started. "What? What didn't he need?"

The old man wouldn't say.

"I won't tell anyone," Molly promised.

You'll take it.

"No, I won't!"

But he seemed unconvinced, his face suddenly that of a sullen child.

"Why would I want it?" she said. "I'm magical, remember? I can make anything, any old time: money, rings. . . ."

The old man shook his head, a knowing expression on his face. Then with fumbling fingers he reached into the leather bag he wore strapped to his belt. Finding what he was searching for, he grinned, displaying three brown teeth, one of them broken.

"You're wasting my time, you know. Either show it to me or don't. It's of no concern to me."

He pulled his hand out of the bag, but he still kept his fingers curled around whatever it was he held. Then slowly he loosened his grip. Molly leaned in and stared.

At first she took it for a giant opal and was calculating what it must be worth—a stone like that could be the centerpiece of a great king's crown. She could see right into its heart, as you can see the pebbles on the bottom of a clear, deep spring. Only this wasn't the pale transparency of water; it was alive with color—deep blues and brilliant greens, with tiny flashes of red. And it didn't just capture the light as even the finest jewels do—this stone had its *own light*. It glowed like a candle.

The old man closed his fingers around it again. Molly thought hard.

"Did William make that?"

Aye. He were magical, like I said.

"What's it for? What does it do?"

William talked to it. Muttering all the time, he was. Having conversations.

"He had conversations with a stone?"

No. He squinted, trying to remember. *More like talking to people who was far away. Old friends, it sounded like.*

"And they answered back? Could you hear them?"

No, but he could.

"That's very magical indeed."

Yeh. I just thought it was pretty.

"It is. It's beautiful."

But now . . . His face brightened. He took his balled fist, still clutching the opal, and pressed it to his lips and then to his eyes. *I can see you and speak to you.*

"Yes."

Ain't never happened afore. That's how come I know you be one of 'em.

"This place," she said. "Harrowsgode. Do you know where it is?"

Up north.

"Where, up north?"

By the sea.

"Due north? How far?"

He seemed distracted now, troubled. *I shouldn't of took it. I shouldn't of.* He rocked slowly back and forth, humming a tuneless melody, not looking at her anymore.

Finally Molly left him and returned to the front of the shop, where Master Frears was making a drawing for Stephen on fine vellum. The picture showed a lidded cup with rubies around the base. He'd gone to the trouble of painting the stones in red, which is how she knew what they were. It was a handsome piece, and the drawing was fine. But it wasn't a Loving Cup.

Stephen gave her a questioning glance.

"We're leaving," she said. "Say something polite."

"That's it, then? Back to Westria?"

"On the contrary. We're going to Harrowsgode, where my grandfather was born. *That's* where we'll find a real Loving Cup."

"Ah," said Stephen. "And where exactly is that?"

"North."

And when Stephen raised his eyebrows, hoping for more, "By the sea," she added.

❧ 5 ❧

North, by the Sea

THE LANDLORD AT THE INN had never heard of Harrowsgode. He hadn't thought there were any cities in the northlands at all. The region was said to be barren and wild, with just the occasional village, maybe a few sheep and goats on the hillsides. They *might* come across an inn or tavern along the way, but probably not. He advised them to take along plenty of provisions.

The north of Austlind proved to be everything the landlord had described, and more. Before the first day's ride was ended, the terrain had grown desolate and rocky, with nothing but the occasional decrepit cottage and a rutted path for a road. And with so little grass for sheep and goats to graze upon, the hillsides were bare.

Lord Mayhew rode ahead of them, keeping a sizable distance between himself and the others. If he could so much as hear the sound of their voices, he'd give his horse a nudge with his spurs. He'd been cold and aloof from the start. But since Faers-Wigan, he'd progressed from aloof to sullen, brooding, and hostile.

It was Molly's proposal—that they should head off into the wastelands of the north, with no real directions, in search of a city that might not exist, to buy a fancy cup for the king—that had done it. He'd refused to go, firmly and absolutely, till Molly finally called his bluff.

"All right," she'd said with a shrug, "then we'll just have to go on our own. But good luck explaining to the king why you came back to Westria without us, the people he'd sent you to protect."

It had been heavy-handed, Molly knew; no doubt she'd made an enemy for life. But she didn't really see that she'd had a choice. Alaric wanted an alliance with Cortova, and to get it he needed the cup. It would have been so much easier if Mayhew had known the importance of their mission. But he didn't. Mayhew couldn't be trusted.

She asked Stephen about it later, and he'd agreed she'd done the right thing. "Though for a while there I was afraid he'd break with us entirely, go home, and do God knows what—start an insurrection or something. He felt so strongly about it; and he's accustomed to giving orders, not taking them."

"Especially from a trumped-up—"

"From anyone, Molly. Even the king. But Mayhew, for his many faults, is a man of honor. He's a knight, and a great one, trained since childhood to give everything he has to the task he's been assigned. Usually that means risking great bodily harm, but in this case it was harder: he had to lay down his pride and go against his firm convictions. Few men of his stature would have done it, but Mayhew did. I'm still thinking about that, but it gives me hope.

"But you've stirred him up. You know how it is when our horses cross a stream: they kick up mud and silt from the bottom, and the water turns cloudy? Then after a while it settles, and the water is clear again? That's how it is with Mayhew. Let's leave him alone for a while and let the anger subside."

"I'll do my best not to annoy him in any way."

"I think that would be very wise."

On their fifth day of wandering in the wilderness, they left the barren plain and started to climb. The air grew crisp and clear again, the dull brown landscape giving way to green. And straight ahead of them loomed a seemingly endless range of mountains.

For the first time Molly began to wonder if she'd imagined all that business about the blind man, and the magical stone, and the city to the north, by the sea. If so, then she had failed Alaric utterly and absolutely, while making Mayhew even more resentful than before and embarrassing herself past bearing.

Then, late in the day, they came quite unexpectedly upon a tidy village. It even had an inn of sorts—small, but remarkably clean. After nights of sleeping on the ground wrapped in their cloaks for warmth and using their saddlebags for pillows, they would sleep indoors on real beds.

The landlord sent a lad up to their rooms with towels and bowls of steaming water so they could wash before coming down to dinner. And as summer nights were cool in the highlands, he'd built a roaring fire in the hall and brought a pitcher of warm, spiced ale to their table. They began to hope that the food might even be good.

"One travels," Stephen said, "and one comes to expect certain things. Occasionally one is surprised."

"Yes," agreed Mayhew with something approaching a smile, "it's a pleasant change. Did you ask the landlord about Harrowsgode?"

"I did. It's in a valley on the other side of those mountains."

"He's heard of it, then? Good. How do we get there? I've been staring at that blasted range for days, and for the life of me I can't see a pass or a road of any kind."

"The landlord couldn't tell me. Apparently no one ever goes there."

"And why is that?" There was an edge to his voice that said he was sure he wasn't going to like the answer.

"Because . . ." Stephen paused and sighed, his face wiped clean of expression. "It is an evil place, and all who enter the valley are turned to stone."

Silence followed, each of them trying to digest this curious morsel of information.

"How does he know that," asked the logical Tobias, "if he's never been there?"

"It's common knowledge, part of the local folklore for hundreds of years. There are actual stone people, right there at the entrance to the valley, for anyone to see."

"Oh, pish," said Winifred.

"I'm just telling you what the fellow said."

"And this *entrance* to the valley, the way *in*—that isn't part of the folklore?"

"Unfortunately not. But it stands to reason that if

the people here know about the city and fear it as they do, then someone from this village must have gone there once, however many years ago, and come back with fanciful tales. It has to be close. And I doubt he climbed over the mountains. There must be a way in."

"Well if there is, it's bloody impossible to see. And unless there's a road leading to it—which there won't be, since no one ever goes there—we'll be traveling blind."

Tobias cleared his throat and said, "Um."

"Um, what?" said Mayhew.

"The raven. I think he knows. I think he's been leading us there this whole time."

Nobody moved then; nobody spoke. All eyes turned toward Mayhew, waiting for him to object—strongly and with curses. But he just stared into the fire, nodding slightly.

"Yes," he finally said, laughing darkly. "We *do* still have that bloody raven."

⌁ ⌁

As they feared, no road led north from the village, not even the trace of an overgrown path. They had nothing to guide them now but the large black bird that continued to fly toward the mountains, never very far ahead. Then, after hours of riding in anxious silence, when the sun was well up in the sky and the dew was gone from the grass, the raven banked sharply to the left. As they followed, the land sloped down into a narrow gully, rather like a dry riverbed; then suddenly the path veered off again to the right and entered a narrow canyon.

No one could have seen it, even at close range, because it ran at an angle, looking like nothing more than another ridge of rock. Yet there it was: two massive walls of honey-gold stone rising so high they had to crane their necks to see a slender strip of sky and so close together they could spread their arms and almost touch both sides. It was as though an angel had sliced through that mountain with his heavenly sword.

In single file they entered the dark, narrow space, the horses treading carefully on the rocky canyon floor.

"I'll bet this runs like a torrent when it rains," Tobias said.

"I'm sure it does," Stephen agreed. "It's a good thing the sky is clear."

"Weather changes sometimes," muttered Winifred.

Now the gorge grew narrower still; their knees and the toes of their boots brushed against the walls. Molly hated close spaces and began to feel uneasy, imagining dead ends and freak thunderstorms, a great wall of water rushing toward them. . . .

"We're almost there," Tobias called from behind her. "Notice the light."

"What about the light?"

"There's more of it than there was before, especially on the right-hand wall. That means it's shining in from the left. Soon we'll turn and you'll see the opening."

And so it was. The space between the walls *did* grow wider. Then they made a slight turn to the left and saw straight ahead of them an opening onto a broad, rocky shelf. Mayhew dismounted and handed his reins to Stephen. Then he walked to the rim and looked down. He stood there for a while, unmoving—and then he laughed.

"What?" they all cried as one.

"People," he said. "Turned to stone."

Molly slid down from her horse and joined him on the rim. A switchback trail led down from the ledge to the valley below; it passed through a strange cluster of rock formations, humanlike and as tall as giants, with rounded heads and curved shoulders dropping down on all sides like flowing robes. From the top of one of those enormous heads there sprouted a delicate pine like a feather in a gentleman's cap.

And there it was—protected by ghoulish guardians,

nestled in a lush valley with a backdrop of another range of mountains and beyond it the sea—a great walled city, larger than Castleton and far more handsome. The sunlight danced off tall spires, slate roofs, and hundreds of glazed windows. A river, beginning as a waterfall in the western mountains, flowed under the walls and into the city itself. There it fanned out into a web of small canals crossed by little bridges, finally coming together again on the other side and then traveling under the walls a second time, filling the wide moat and then flowing on into a village, watering the fields, and finally winding off into the distant forest, where it was lost from sight.

"Well," Mayhew said, "I believe we have found your Harrowsgode. Shall we go down and get ourselves a cup?"

From above, the raven swooped down into the valley, a message they all understood.

Taking their horses by the reins, with slow and careful steps, they followed.

❧ 6 ❧

Hue and Cry

ON THE VALLEY FLOOR, the land spread out around them in a chessboard of parti-color fields. Neatly thatched and whitewashed houses—with their bee-hives and dovecotes, sheepfolds and henhouses, pigpens and kitchen plots—alternated with orchards, vineyards, gristmills, and dairies, and mile after mile of wheat and barley, swaying in the wind, touched with gold by the afternoon sun.

"Oh, my stars!" said Winifred. "What a magical place!"

Stephen grinned. "Not magical. Just a trick of the light. That, and very good husbandry."

The harvest had just begun. Teams of workers were out in the fields swinging their sickles rhythmically, spreading the new-cut wheat, speckled with the last of the wildflowers, out on the stubble to dry in the sun. They stopped their work to stare as the strangers rode by.

The streets of the little town were neatly cobbled, with no horse flop on the road, no filth in the gutters, no animals running wild. And the shops were uncommonly plentiful for a village of that size. They passed a cobbler, a tanner, a weaver, a tailor, two bakers, a cooper, an ironmonger, and a butcher—and that was just the high street. What else there might be on the side lanes could only be imagined.

There weren't many shoppers on the street—most were probably busy with the harvest—but those who were, together with the merchants, also stopped to stare.

"Stephen," Molly whispered, "I think they're afraid of us."

"It's possible. I doubt they see strangers very often."

"We should smile so as not to look threatening."

"Molly, my dear, I don't believe you could look threatening if you tried."

Tobias laughed at that, rather louder than was absolutely necessary. Molly made a face at him.

They continued through the village and out again, where the street opened into a broad avenue leading to the moat that gave added protection to the city—at which point the road ended. The drawbridge was up.

"That's bloody inconvenient," Mayhew grumbled. "Do you suppose it's been raised on our account?"

"Maybe they keep it up all the time," Stephen said. "No one ever comes here, remember?"

"All right, let's turn back. We'll have to ask one of the villagers how to get inside the city—though who's likely to tell us, I can't imagine. They gape at us like we're carrying the plague."

"I saw a wineshop back there," Winifred said. "Near the square, on a lane to the right. The sign over the door showed a bunch of grapes, and there was a trestle table out in the yard under a big old tree."

"Good. A wineshop is perfect. Stephen, you and Winifred go down there and order yourselves some dinner. Ask the appropriate questions. You know Austlinder."

"All right," Stephen said. "But I think I should take off my sword. Nobody wears them here."

"I noticed that, too. But in case they're not as peaceful as they seem, I'll keep watch from the other end of the street. If you get your hackles up, give me a sign."

Stephen unbuckled his scabbard and handed it to Mayhew. Then he offered Winifred his arm and they sauntered back up the high street like an old married couple out for a Sunday stroll. Mayhew left Molly and Tobias to mind the horses while he skirted the edge of the town in search of a watching spot.

They found a small copse of trees and tied up the horses. Tobias tossed his wineskin to Molly, unfastened the bag of provisions, and took out some bread and cheese. Side by side, they sat in the shade, eating their rustic dinner.

Kerrokk!

"Oh!" Molly cried, scrambling to her feet and searching among the leafy branches. "Where are you hiding, raven dear?"

Kerrokk!

"Ah, there you are!"

Having shown himself, the bird now took flight, rising high into the air, making a wide circle over a cluster of animal pens, then landing on a distant fence post. From there he called to them, his grating voice loud and insistent.

They didn't hesitate. Grabbing Molly's hand, Tobias led her down the path that followed the fence line, turning left the first chance he got, then right again. The raven was on the far side of the enclosure, where a large black bull stood with his back to them, his head low and at an angle. With the tip of one horn he was prodding something that lay on the ground.

It was a man, they realized, and he was almost certainly dead.

Tobias dropped Molly's hand and ran. It wasn't till he'd turned the second corner that he got a proper look at the body: crumpled and stained with blood, the bull standing over it, nudging, nudging with the vicious point of his horn.

Tobias picked up a large rock and threw it at the bull, but he missed. It'd been too heavy, and his hand was trembling. Molly handed him a smaller one, and this time his aim was true. The beast stepped back, fixing them with a venomous stare. When the next rock hit the mark again, the bull turned and slowly walked away.

"Warn me if he's coming back," Tobias said, climbing over the fence and squatting beside the figure: a young man, maybe seventeen or eighteen, his fine saffron doublet ripped and soaked with gore. Tobias touched a cheek and found it cold. Then he licked the palm of his hand and held it over the boy's mouth and nose. Like putting a finger to the wind, he would feel the slightest movement of air. There wasn't any.

"He's dead."

"I know, Tobias. I can see that from here."

"Should I move him, so the bull won't—?"

"No," Molly said. "We must raise the hue and cry. And the coroner needs to see him as he lies so it'll be plain to everyone what happened. But first, get out of that blasted pen. I'll get some more rocks. We can keep the bull away till help arrives."

They hallooed till their throats were sore, and before long a man arrived. He stayed just long enough to size up the situation, and gape at the strangers, before running back to summon the coroner and the four nearest neighbors as required by law.

The neighbors, all women, were the first to come; they were followed by a man whose carroty hair sprung out from his head on all sides like a rusty dandelion puff. Unlike the women, who were more interested in Molly and Tobias than in the poor dead boy, the man was visibly distressed. He had to lean on a fence post to keep from collapsing.

"The boy's father," Tobias whispered.

"No," Molly said. "The owner of the bull."

"Why do you say that?"

"The boy is rich, for one thing—look at his clothes—whereas that man is a peasant. And they don't resemble each other at all."

Tobias looked at the weeping man, with his

peculiar hair and weak chin, then down at the hand-some youth. "You're right," he said quietly. "The boy looks nothing at all like that man. . . ."

His thought sounded unfinished, so she asked, "What, Tobias?"

"He looks exactly like you."

More people came. Ropes were brought and the bull was restrained at the far end of the paddock. Finally the coroner arrived (he was also the village butcher, by the looks of his apron), and the crowd gave way to let him pass. He climbed over the fence, as Tobias had done, and came to the same conclusion.

"He's one of theirs," the butcher said. "It's not our business. I'll go to the tower and have them sound the alarm. Meanwhile, someone call up to the ramparts and tell them what's happened. Say they need to send out their coroner."

"Let's go," Tobias said. "This is none of our business, either."

But apparently it was, because the crowd was quite insistent that they stay right where they were.

"Are we under arrest?" Molly whispered.

"No. I think they need us to testify at the trial."

"Why should there be a trial? It was an accident."

"I don't know. Maybe the owner of the bull is being held responsible."

"But it wasn't his fault."

Tobias shrugged. "We'll find out, I guess."

"I wonder where . . ."

Molly turned to one of the women then and asked in fractured Austlinder, "Where we is for this thing we go?"

"The trial?"

"Yes."

"Harrowsgode," she said, pointing.

Molly smiled.

7

The Trial

THE ENTRY GATE OF Harrowsgode didn't open onto the street, as it would in any other city. Instead, they came first to a small atrium, where they waited while the gate was locked, the portcullis lowered, and the drawbridge raised. Then they waited some more. Though there was another door in the little room, the guard made no move to open it.

"They're summoning the court and a jury," said Stephen, who'd been permitted to accompany Molly and Tobias and act as their translator. "They assure us it won't take long."

"Good," Molly said. "It's bloody close in here."

The villagers stood clustered together, as far from the strangers as the limited space would allow; they talked in low voices and stared at Molly.

"Why do they keep looking at me like that?" she whispered to Stephen. "What are they saying?"

"They think you must be one of the Harrowsgode folk. They say you look just like them, and your skin glows the same as theirs does."

"Oh, horse flop!"

"You asked me what they were saying. You do resemble them, though."

"I suppose," she said. "But I don't glow. Not in the least."

Tobias studied her, head at an angle as if trying to judge whether she glowed or not. Molly flicked his arm and gave him a look.

"Stephen," he asked, "did anyone mention who exactly is being tried?"

"You really don't know?"

"Would I have asked if I did?"

"It's the *bull*, Tobias."

"No!"

"Yes. I've seen a pig hanged for wandering into a cottage, upsetting a cradle, and devouring an infant."

"Lord, Stephen, that's horrible!"

"Which part?"

"All of it. As for hanging a pig—it's absurd. It was just a beast doing what beasts do. Surely it's the parents who ought to be punished for letting the pig run free and leaving the infant alone with the door open."

"The law is not always wise, Tobias, and the bull is indeed being tried for murder."

"Will they hang it?" Molly wondered. "I can't imagine."

"Ha! What a scaffold *that* would be. No, they'll probably slit its throat, then destroy the meat so none may partake of its evil flesh."

"Gaw!"

"I thought you'd be amazed."

The room had grown uncomfortably warm, and the smell of so many sweating bodies was strong. Molly leaned against Tobias—the top of her head just reaching his collarbone—and groaned. "How much longer can this possibly take? It's hard to breathe in here."

"You've been in worse places," he said, and she agreed.

Finally they heard a key turning in the lock; and the door swung open to reveal not the city but a great, cavernous hall, with floors and walls of stone and a high ceiling supported by massive wooden beams. At one end was a dais covered with a velvet cloth. And built into the two side walls were long benches with wooden back rests six feet high and decoratively carved at the top. They were led to the nearest bench and told to sit down.

The court was already assembled. The judge sat on a raised chair at the center of the dais dressed in a scarlet gown, like a bishop on his throne. To his left and right were the barristers, dressed in similar robes. There was also a scribe and, on the far edge of the dais, an official holding a staff. On the bench directly across from them sat the jury.

It was the first time Molly had seen so many Harrowsgode folk gathered together—and indeed they *did* all look remarkably alike. Despite differences in age, dress, and social standing, they might have been one great family—the wealthy uncle, his up-and-coming nephews, and the poor relations—all of the same seed, however differently they'd grown. And it wasn't just the dark curls and the pale gray eyes. There *was* something about them that was bright and fresh: the clear skin with its perfect sheen picking up the light from the windows overhead and the torches along the walls.

Molly studied her own familiar hands, turning them palms up, then palms down. They didn't seem exceptional in any way. Tobias, who sat beside her, noticed. He reached over and took one of those ordinary hands and kept it in his. She found this a comfort.

Stephen, on her other side, leaned over and

whispered in her ear. "They don't intend to let us into the city at all. When the trial is over, they'll take us out again."

"How do you know that?"

"One of the neighbors told me. Harrowsgode is a closed city. Not even their villagers may enter, which explains this room, I suppose. This is where they bring their crops, and get paid, and so on."

"That's a problem, then."

"Maybe not. If they regard you as one of their own, they might make an exception. They've all noticed the resemblance. So when the time comes, you need to step forward quickly and try to get someone's attention, tell him your grandfather was born here, that you've come back searching for relatives—that sort of thing."

"But who?"

"I don't know yet. Let's see what happens during the trial."

There came a great thumping noise; the official with the staff was pounding the floor of the dais, calling the people to attention.

"The court is now is session," he cried. "May justice be done!"

"Know ye," said the judge, "that we are gathered here to rule on the death of our brother, Kort Gunnarson. Master Coroner, please give your report."

The coroner stood, made a respectful bow, then described the scene of the crime: the position of the body, the nature of the wounds, and the presence of blood on the bull's horns. He was questioned briefly by the two barristers, then the coroner bowed a second time and resumed his seat.

"Witnesses next," whispered Stephen.

"Tobias, Lord Worthington of Westria," called the judge. "Please stand and give your testimony."

Tobias squeezed Molly's hand, then released it and got to his feet. "I not speak you language well. Friend Stephen with me help," he said.

"That will be allowed," said the judge. "Master Einar, you may begin the prosecution."

"Lord Worthington," Master Einar said, "you arrived here this morning from outside the valley?"

"That's correct," Tobias said.

"And you happened to come upon the body of the deceased?"

"Yes. We were some distance away, so we went to investigate."

"And what did you find?"

"A young man lying near the fence covered in

blood. A bull was probing the body with his horn. We drove the beast away with stones. Then I went inside the enclosure and determined that the boy was dead."

"Did you see anyone else nearby? A man with a weapon, perhaps? Someone running off into the wheat fields in a suspicious manner?"

"No."

"Just the bull."

"Yes."

"What did you do then?"

"We gave the hue and cry. Someone came, then he notified the four neighbors and the owner of the bull. The village coroner too."

"Did you notice, by chance, if there was any blood on the bull's horns?"

"I heard the coroner say there was. I didn't see it myself."

"Have you anything further to add?"

"No."

"Remain standing please, Lord Worthington," said the judge. "Master Pieter will speak for the defense."

Master Einar took his seat and Master Pieter now stepped forward.

"Lord Worthington," he said, "when you and Lady Marguerite first noticed the body, was it inside the bull's enclosure or out?"

"Inside."

"When you drove the animal off and climbed in to check on the boy, did you move the body at all?"

"No. Since he was already dead and there was nothing to be done for him, we felt it was best to leave the scene as it was—for the coroner, you understand."

"Yes. You did the proper thing. That's all I have for now."

Master Pieter returned to his seat, and Tobias sat down. Now it was Molly's turn.

"Lady Marguerite," Master Einar said, "you were with Lord Worthington during the entire time in question?"

"Yes, I was."

"And did you see anything that hasn't already been mentioned?"

"Not really."

"No one running away from the scene? You didn't stumble upon a dropped weapon?"

She shook her head.

"Just the bull standing over the victim, jabbing the body with his horn."

"Yes."

"Thank you."

That was it? As Einar sat down and Pieter took his place, Molly started to panic. As the second witness, with nothing new to add, she was clearly being dispensed with quickly. And this would be her last chance to mention her grandfather. She'd just have to keep her wits about her and work the information in somehow, no matter how silly and irrelevant it seemed.

"Please tell me, Lady Marguerite," Master Pieter began, "how it is you came to our valley. Were you lost?"

Molly blinked. He had given her the perfect opening!

"No, Master Pieter, we were not lost. We were searching for Harrowsgode most particularly."

"And why is that?"

"My grandfather, a silversmith of great renown, was said to have come from this city." Stephen struggled with a grin as he translated this for the court. It really had been too easy. "He went by the name of William Harrows and lived his latter days in the town of Faers-Wigan, but I believe he—and I—have family here. I came with my companions to seek them out."

There—it was done! Her foot was firmly wedged in the door.

"I rather suspected as much, my lady," Master Pieter said. "You greatly resemble us Harrowsgode folk."

"Please stick to the defense, Master Pieter," said the judge.

"Of course. My apologies for straying off the topic. Now, Lady Marguerite, your friend Lord Worthington said you drove the bull away with stones. Can you tell me why you did that?"

"So Tobias could get into the enclosure to look after the boy, to see if he still lived."

"And you couldn't do that while the bull was near?"

"Of course not. It wouldn't be safe."

"But it was safe where you were, outside the enclosure?"

"Yes."

He nodded thoughtfully as if this were a tricky puzzle. "Normally, if you saw a bull inside a pen surrounded by a strong fence, would you be alarmed?"

"I don't understand your question."

"Well, suppose you saw a bull walking down the street or in the fishmonger's shop—would you be alarmed then?"

"Anyone would."

"Because?"

"It would be dangerous." Where was he going with this? Everything he said was so obvious it didn't bear mentioning at all.

"Is the bull not also dangerous within his enclosure?"

"Yes, but there's a stout fence to keep him in,

whereas on the street or in a shop there's nothing to restrain him from doing harm."

"Very good. Now tell me—you seem a clever young lady—do you think a bull has the right to exist? Keeping in mind that he is a dangerous beast."

"I should hope so—else we'd have no cows or calves." There was a titter of laughter from the jury.

"Master Pieter?" said the judge, a warning note in his voice.

"Please have patience a little longer, my lord; I am about to make my point."

"Make it soon. We haven't got all day."

"Thank you, my lord, I shall. So would it be fair to say, Lady Marguerite, that the bull should be allowed to dwell alongside his masters—we of the human race—so long as he is confined and can do us no harm?"

"Yes. Though in this particular case—"

"I was just getting to that. I believe we all agree that the bull, to exist at all, must have some place of his own in which to live; that place is within his enclosure. The humans who control him, and use him for their purposes, live everywhere else. Correct?"

Molly nodded, entranced.

"So the young man, by climbing into his pen, was *trespassing*, was he not?"

Ah. She saw where he was going now. "It was

certainly a foolish thing to do."

"No one questions that it was foolish. But had he the *right*?"

Molly shrugged.

"A king may not cross the threshold of the humblest man's cottage unless he is bid to enter. Is it not so with our bull, who has no choice but to stay where he is put and no choice in his warlike nature, which was endowed by his creator? Can we truly call it murder when the bull was defending his home?"

"I . . . suppose . . ."

"That was a rhetorical question, lady," said the judge. "You are not expected to answer."

After that it went quickly, a mere formality. The neighbors had nothing of interest to say. The owner begged for the life of his bull, as it was a valuable animal and the loss would tax his household greatly. The prosecutor and the defense each came forward and summed up the case. Then the jury rose and the official with the staff led them across the hall to a room where they could discuss the case in private and come to their decision.

"I think," whispered Stephen, "Master Pieter is our man."

"I think so, too," Molly said. "Wasn't it amazing how he led me directly to the very thing I'd wanted to say? I was afraid I would never get the chance."

"He did it on purpose. Whether out of curiosity or for some other reason, I cannot guess. But for sure you may safely approach him. I would not be surprised if he came to you himself."

"Nor would I. Listen, Stephen, I think he might be more open if I speak to him alone."

"Can you manage the language?"

"I understand a lot of what I hear now so long as the words aren't too fancy. Speaking is harder, of course—"

"It always is."

"But I think I can make myself clear. You and Tobias stay nearby, but not too close. I'll nod to you if I need help."

"All right. Have you thought of what you will say to him?"

"Stephen, I've thought of nothing else since we came into this place."

❦

The decision must have been an easy one; minutes later the door opened and the jury filed back out.

"Who is your spokesman?" asked the judge.

"I am, Your Honor," said a heavyset man.

"Then give us your verdict, please."

"Your Honor, we find the beast innocent of murderous intent."

"So be it. We thank you for your service."

The official struck the dais three times with his staff, then suddenly everyone was in motion. The jury rose to their feet, the judge and barristers stepped down, and the official headed over to the witness bench to lead the villagers out. But Master Pieter didn't follow the others to the far side of the room, where they stood in a knot by the great double doors that almost certainly led into the city. Instead, he remained in the middle of the room, apparently waiting for her.

"Now!" said Stephen. "Go!"

Molly grabbed her saddle pack and hurried over to the barrister.

"Master Pieter," she said. "I talk you, please?"

"Of course. I would be delighted." He said this in flawless Westrian.

"You speak my language?"

"Oh, yes. There are many in Harrowsgode who do. We are a scholarly people."

"Good," Molly said. "For I am *not* scholarly in the least, and I've been making rather a muddle of speaking Austlinder."

"Lady," he said, brushing this aside, "I want you to know that you are welcome here. Harrowsgode is, in the truest sense, your home. And there is much I am eager to tell you—about your family, and about our people. If you'll just wait here with me until the others have gone, I'll take you into the city."

"But what about my friends?"

"I'm sorry. They are not permitted."

"Why? They traveled all this way with me so I could find my grandfather's people; now we're here and you say they can't go inside?"

"Harrowsgode isn't an open city. Only our people may enter. You are one of us; they are not."

"They won't do you any harm."

"It's interesting that you say that since you came accompanied by a knight, and all your men were armed."

"That had nothing at all to do with you," she said, wondering how he knew so much. "Lord Mayhew— the knight—just came along to protect us on the road. I don't care if he stays behind now that we're here. But I do need Winifred for propriety; she's my lady companion. And Stephen is my translator. And Tobias—"

"We will find you a lady companion, one of your own kind. And as you will have noticed, I speak your language. You won't need a translator here."

She felt a rush of panic; her face went damp with sweat. She looked into Pieter's gray eyes, her desperation unmasked, and said in a voice that was deep and urgent: "Then I must have Tobias."

"But, lady—"

"Please believe me: I want to go with you into the city, but *I will not go without him*."

"Why—are you betrothed?"

Her breath caught. She paused. She heard herself say yes.

"You are very young. Was this arranged by your father?"

She paused again.

"Yes," she said. "Yes, it was."

Oh, how she choked on that dreadful lie—as if her father gave a goose's fart about whom she married, or if she even married at all! Why, she hadn't so much as laid eyes on the man since she was seven, when he'd decided it was time she earned her own bread and dragged her off to Dethemere Castle to work as a scullery maid.

"You are aware, my lady, that no maid can be compelled to marry against her will—not by her father, or anyone else. That is the law."

"I have no desire to break my bond. Tobias is my dearest friend—and besides, we are sworn to each other."

"Already sworn? Truly?"

The villagers had left the room by then. Now the official came back for the foreigners—Stephen, Tobias, and Molly—who seemed to be lingering.

"Not the tall one," Pieter said to the official. "Lord Worthington and the lady will remain here. But you may take the other one out." The official raised his eyebrows in surprise. But as no explanation was forthcoming, he did as he was told.

"Lord Worthington," Pieter called, waving Tobias over. "Will you come and join us, please."

Tobias had been staring dumbfounded as Stephen was ushered out of the room. Now he came forward, looking to Molly for assurance that everything was all right. She responded with something between a twitch and a wink.

"My lord," Pieter said, "you know that Lady Marguerite is descended from the folk of this city. She testified to that effect not an hour ago."

He nodded.

"And so, being one of us, she is granted free entrance here."

Tobias had always been good at silence. He proved this once again. He waited for the rest of it as unmoving as a mountain, looking down at the little barrister with solemn eyes.

"You, of course, would not normally be permitted beyond this room. We're a closed city. Our gates stay shut, our drawbridge raised, unless business is to be done with our villagers. Even then they may only come so far as this chamber and never through those doors."

Tobias still waited. He scarcely seemed to breathe. "However . . ."

Heaven help me, Molly thought, *here it comes!*

"The lady has expressed the strongest unwillingness to go unless you, her betrothed"—Tobias blanched—"should be allowed to come with her. And as we will never turn away one of our people who has returned to us, we will make an exception and allow it."

"Master Pieter," Tobias said, his face now transformed by a foolish grin, "as *her betrothed*, I am most happy, most grateful, truly honored to be admitted into the city where my future wife's family—"

"Tobias?"

"Yes, my dearest?"

"You have said enough, I think."

The outer gates were shut and bolted. The grinding of chains said the portcullis was down and the drawbridge was being raised. Molly glanced over at the crowd by the door that led into Harrowsgode: the judge, the prosecutor, the official, the scribe, and the jury. All were watching them with unvarnished curiosity.

"Excuse me," Pieter said. "I must go and explain.

Please don't worry. It'll be all right."

"Control yourself," Molly hissed when Pieter had gone.

"It's very hard to do, sweetheart. Under the circumstances."

She covered her mouth to hide a grin. "Well, you must try. This is important."

"I know, my darling."

"If you darling-dearest me one more time, I'll tell him the truth, and he'll send you packing."

"No you won't. But all the same, I promise to behave. I was just overcome by a wave of giddiness. I'm completely recovered now. Rather bored by it, actually."

"Good. We're sworn, just so you know. My father made the arrangements."

"Your father? *Really?*"

"Tobias!"

"He's coming back now, Molly. You'd best control yourself."

The official produced a ring of keys and unlocked the door. The jury filed out, followed by the prosecutor and the scribe. Only the judge remained—standing in the open doorway, backlit by the warm light of a late summer afternoon—glaring at them. The man with the keys waited.

Something wasn't right. Molly wondered if the barrister actually had the authority to let them in. Certainly the judge disapproved. But Pieter was standing his ground. Finally the judge shook his head, slowly and solemnly as if in warning, then turned on his heel and left.

Pieter watched him go. At last, his face flushed and his voice dark with feeling, he turned to them and spoke. "He's old-fashioned in his views. I respect him, but in this case he is wrong. We can never, ever turn away one of our own—and a child of the Magnus line!" His voice broke and he cleared his throat. "He will be gone now. No need to fear any unpleasantness. Will you follow me?"

Just as they were about to step over the threshold, Pieter paused. "My lady," he said solemnly, "welcome home."

❦ 8 ❧

The Tale of King Magnus

PIETER'S OFFICE WAS a pleasant chamber with a wide bank of leadlight windows looking out onto the great courtyard of the university. Everything about the room was tidy and bright, the personal space of a thoughtful man who was not lavish but who loved pretty things.

He introduced them to his mother, who sat by the window with her needlework. She was small and elegant like her son, her dark hair streaked with silver. "Mother will serve as your lady companion for now," he said to Molly. "Later we will make other arrangements. It's not our custom here, but I wouldn't want you to feel uncomfortable."

Molly wished like the devil that she'd never brought the whole thing up. It had just been an excuse to bring Winifred.

Pieter led them over to a pair of handsome chairs facing a large wooden desk. "Please," he said. "Make yourselves comfortable." Then he went around the desk and sat across from them.

"If you will excuse me for just a moment, I must make some arrangements. I promise it won't take long. Then we will talk."

He took several sheets of vellum out of a drawer and laid them on the desk. Then he unstopped his inkwell, dipped the point of his pen into it, and began to write, taking great pains with his swirls and loops. When he was finished, he blotted the ink, turned the paper over, and addressed it on the top edge. But he didn't fold and seal it as was done in other places. He just rolled it up and tied it with a ribbon.

Now he took up his pen again and started on a second letter. When he was done with that one, he wrote a third. At last he flashed a smile at them that said *Almost done!* and rang a little brass bell that sat on his desk. An assistant popped out of an adjoining room, and Pieter handed him the letters.

"Deliver the one to the Council first, then the one to the Magnussons. After that you can go to

Neargate. It's a lot of ground to cover, so you may take the spinner."

The boy's face brightened.

"And, Robbin, if you damage it, I'll take it out of your hide. You understand?"

"Yes, Master," the boy said. "I'll bring it back as good as new." He hurried out, shutting the door behind him with exaggerated care.

"There," Pieter said. "Everything is now in motion. Like the heavens," he added with a chuckle. "Now draw your chairs closer, if you will. While we wait, I have something to show you."

He brought out a much larger roll of vellum and spread it out on the table. As it wanted to curl back up again, he set little velvet bags filled with sand on each of the corners to hold it down.

They leaned forward to look at the scroll. It was covered with curvy letters, some in writing so small you couldn't possibly read it even if you knew how. There were lines connecting one word to the next and little pictures rendered in color. Everything was embellished with gleaming gold paint.

"That's beautiful," Tobias said. "I never saw anything like it."

"Well," said Pieter, "thank you for saying so. It's my own little project, not anything to compare with the great Map of the People that is kept in Harrowsgode Hall. But it will suffice for our purposes."

"*You* made that?" Molly asked, astonished.

"Well, yes, I did. I rather fancied myself an artist in my youth, but there's little call for such skills in my profession. So I entertain myself with a brush and pen—in my spare time, you understand. Now let me tell you about it; I brought it out for a reason.

"Here at the top you see three thrones, and upon them sit three kings. This one, whose throne is raised above the others, let us call him the Great King for the sake of simplicity. He was the father of the two below. We shall come to them in a moment.

"Now the Great King was strong in war, very powerful and clever with weapons. When he was still a young man, the crown hardly warm from the touch of his brow, he gathered an army and sailed across the waters to conquer our people. That was long ago, hundreds and hundreds of years."

Molly loved a story. She leaned in, her elbows resting on Pieter's desk, for a closer look at the three small images of kings on their thrones: one above, two below; two fair, one dark.

"Now the Great King married a lady of his own race, and she bore him a son, Harald—also several daughters, but they were of no account, for women could not rule. This is Harald: the fair one who sits below his father on your left.

"Now in time the queen died, as queens do, giving birth to yet another daughter; and the Great King married again. Only this time he chose a lady from the conquered race, one of our own. Here is *their* son, on the right, with the dark hair. He was called Magnus.

"Now the Great King loved his second wife, and the son she bore him, more than he loved the first. And when his life's thread had worn thin and was near to breaking, he made his desires known regarding the succession; to the astonishment of all, he chose Magnus as his heir instead of the firstborn son.

"Well, you can imagine what happened after that. It was war all over the kingdom, with Harald, who claimed to be the rightful heir (and surely you can see his point), driving Magnus off the throne, after which the once-conquered people rose up in revolt. Many died in those terrible times.

"And it was all utterly pointless, for Magnus was a mystic and a scholar, not a warrior or a man of the world; he had no desire to rule a country or lead an army. Yet all over the kingdom his people were dying in his name, dying to defend his right to an unwanted throne. So he formally renounced the crown and acknowledged his brother as king.

"But it was already too late. The pot was boiling; everyone was angry—conquered and conquerors alike. *Our* people were convinced that their king had been forced to abdicate. *Their* people were sure the crown had been stolen from the rightful heir.

"Finally Magnus made a proposal. There was a large island belonging to the kingdom called Budenholme, just off the coast. As the soil was poor and rocky, it was mostly uninhabited. Magnus said it was all the land that he would claim. He would go and live there, never to return, but any of his people who wished to follow him must be permitted to do so. He would become the ruler of his own tiny kingdom.

"Harald agreed to this, and provided Magnus with ships to carry everything he and his followers would need to start their new life on the island. Then he left them in peace to live as they wished, just as he had promised.

"But there were others, wild raiders with fast ships who swore allegiance to no king. They noticed that the once-barren island was now sprouting cottages and wheat fields; the hillsides were covered with herds of grazing sheep. And so they came sweeping in time after time, stealing sheep, pigs, grain, and now and then a comely maiden. It was so easy—why, the innocents who lived there didn't even have an army! They had no weapons at all!"

"Horrible!" Molly said.

"Yes, it was. So clearly they would have to find another home, someplace safe, quiet, and remote. But where?

"Magnus needed to consider the matter, and to do this he needed to be alone. So he climbed to the top of the highest hill and built himself a crude little shelter, just enough to keep off the sun and the rain. And there he stayed—we don't know how long—living on nothing but the bread and water that were set outside his door every morning. And during·that time King Magnus had a vision."

Molly gasped.

"He saw a lush valley fed by rivers and guarded by mountains on all four sides, the coastal range dropping precipitously down to the sea. He saw a few peasants living there, growing crops, cut off from the rest of the world since the time before time. He saw dense, honey-colored stone ready to be quarried for building. And he saw his men at the top of soaring cliffs with a system of winches and ropes, hauling their things up from the ships below, animals and bedsteads alike. And best of all, he saw the way in to that sweet, protected spot: a narrow canyon near impossible to find if you didn't know the way, cutting right through the southern mountains.

"When he came back down the hill—ragged and dirty, no doubt, and with a scraggly beard—he told his people to pack up their belongings and get the ships ready to sail. That is how they came to settle in this place and build this beautiful city. It was a labor of many generations, but these walls and these mountains have kept us safe ever since." Pieter took a deep breath, his face glowing with pride.

"That's amazing," Molly said. "What a wonderful story."

"Indeed. And as you shall see, we have created a paradise here, untouched and untroubled by the world."

Molly stared thoughtfully at the great sheet of vellum.

"But what about all the rest of the scroll—that part, and that? All those little pictures and lines?"

"It's a map of our people, showing the leaders of the seven clans, from the time of Magnus to the present generation."

"What does that mean—clans?"

"They grew out of family groups long ago. There would have been a patriarch named Gunnar, for example, who was a great hunter, so his descendants became the Gunnarclan, who now serve as the archers on our ramparts. We don't allow weapons here, as you know, but we have made that one exception. As we are not a warlike people and have no army, we need at least *some* protection. Just in case."

"No army?" said Tobias, astonished.

"We have mountains instead." Pieter smiled. "So, that's the Gunnarclan. In the same way, long ago, there was a man named Stig, who was a sailor. His descendants are the Stiggesclan, from which our Voyagers are chosen. They don't sail in ships, not anymore; but they are the only ones who are permitted to leave our valley and go out into the world—secretly, you understand—to learn of new things and bring back wisdom to our people."

"And you?"

"I'm of the Visenclan. We are scholars, mostly. This is my family line, here."

"But what about the one in the middle? It has more names than the others. And so many lines lead to it, and there's so much gold paint."

Pieter smiled. "That is *your* clan, lady—the descendants of King Magnus."

"Gaw!" cried Tobias, forgetting himself entirely. "You're a royal princess, Molly!"

"Is it true?" she asked.

"In a way. Not exactly. The king's line is here." He

showed them where the Magnus clan had split several times, some lines dying out, a few running side by side all the way to the bottom. "See the little gold crown I have painted here? That's our king, Koenraad; and below him you see his son, Prince Fredrik. You are part of this other line, here. But it's true you are of royal lineage—noble, I believe you'd call it in your country."

Molly was struck speechless. Royal blood—who would have thought it?

Pieter now opened a drawer and took out a strange object. It was like half of a ball made out of glass. He positioned it carefully at the end of her branch of the Magnus line, peering down and adjusting it slightly. "There!" he said. "Don't touch it, lady. Just—it's better if you stand and look straight down. Now tell me, what do you see?".

"Oh, you have made the words larger."

"Not me, the magnifying glass."

"Is it magic?"

"No. It's science, the science of optics. But what I wished you to notice is the word that's being magnified."

"Oh. I don't know how to read."

"That's all right. I'll help you. Now imagine two valleys, side by side." He drew the shape with a finger in the air. "That is the letter *W*."

"But I know that one already!" she cried. "I also know the letter *M*."

"Well, how clever of you!"

She flushed then, hearing her own words and hearing his reply. No doubt he'd meant to be kind, but to say to a man who could read *anything*, a man who knew *all* the letters and could write them down as well—to say *I know* M *and* W as though that were some great accomplishment . . .

"I had a necklace," she explained. "The king of Westria has it now. My grandfather made it as a love-gift for my grandmother, so he worked both of their initials into the design: *M* for *Martha* and *W* for *William*. That's the only reason I know. Otherwise, I'm as ignorant as a toad."

"No you're not. You just haven't had an education. But you're as sharp and clever as any young lady of my acquaintance. Now look again—don't move it; I have it perfectly placed—and tell me what you see."

"The letter *W*."

"Exactly. And combined with the others that follow, it spells out the name William."

"Like my grandfather?"

"That *is* your grandfather, lady."

"Oh." And then, after studying it a while, "But

there's nothing under it, no little lines running down . . ."

"Not yet," Pieter said, turning the scroll around so the top part, with the three kings, was on their side of the table now and the word that said *William* was in front of him. From out of his pocket he pulled a new device—two metallic rings, each holding a circle of glass just as strips of lead hold the panes of a window. The rings of metal and glass were connected by a squiggly bit of wire in the middle.

"Eyeglasses," Pieter said, slipping the squiggly bit onto his nose. "They magnify as the glass dome does, so I can see to work small." Then he sharpened his pen with a knife, wiped it clean with a cloth, and dipped it into the ink.

"You must tell me the names. William begat—?"

"What is 'begat'?"

"William's issue. His children."

"Oh. There was just my mother."

"And her name?"

"Greta."

He nodded and carefully began to write the name on the scroll. When he was done, he drew a remarkably straight line running down from it and looked up again at Molly.

"How would you like to be listed, lady?" His eyes,

as seen through the circles of glass, were distorted.

"You look like a demon in those eyeglasses."

"I assure you I am nothing of the kind. Now how shall I list you? As Marguerite? Or your full title? It'll be tight, but I think I can manage."

Molly pinched her lips and thought. "Not the title, no." She chewed on a fingernail, thinking some more. "Just Molly," she decided. "That's who I really am."

"All right." She watched, scarcely breathing, as he slowly, carefully, made the tiny strokes on the paper that spelled out her name, and enrolled her for all time as one of the people of Harrowsgode.

"Oh, Master Pieter—is that really my name? Tobias, you must come and see!"

"It's wonderful," he said, leaning over to look. "Exactly the way a princess's name ought to be written."

"I'm not a princess," she said, though her face fairly glowed with pleasure.

Just then the assistant returned, closing the door very gently again—no doubt he'd been scolded for slamming it—and handed Pieter a single scroll.

"Only one reply?" he asked. Then, checking to see who'd sent it, "Nothing from the Council?"

"No, Master. They were very busy. They just took the letter and sent me on my way."

"I understand." He opened the scroll and scanned

it quickly, nodding with satisfaction. "What about Richard Strange?" he asked. "Did you not go to Neargate?"

"I did. He's agreed to host the gentleman."

"All right, then," Pieter said to Molly and Tobias. "It grows late, and all is now arranged. Shall we away?"

"Where?"

"To your lodgings. We have no inns in Harrowsgode, as we have no travelers; but you'll be quite comfortable, I promise. Marguerite—excuse me, Molly—you'll be the guest of a near relative, Claus Magnusson, a professor at the university. His father was William's brother, so that would make him a cousin of sorts. The family knows Westrian, so language won't be a problem."

"What about me?" Tobias asked.

"You'll be staying with a gentleman named Richard Strange. He was born in Westria, so he knows the language. I'm sure you'll suit each other splendidly. Now, come. Get your things. Robbin, you take Lord Worthington over to Neargate. I'll see to the lady. Do you want my mother to accompany us?"

"No," Molly said. "It's just a stuffy old custom."

"As you like, my dear. Shall we go?"

And then they were out the door and through the gates of the university, where they parted—she to go one way and he another. It had all happened too fast.

"But how will I see Tobias?" she asked. "We didn't make any plans. I don't even know where he's staying."

"Don't worry. Dr. Magnusson will arrange it. No problem at all."

❧ 9 ❧

The Great Seer

KING KOENRAAD WAS VERY OLD. He was nearly blind, profoundly deaf, and too frail to walk without assistance. He'd completely forgotten his once-beloved queen, dead now these many years; and he didn't recognize Prince Fredrik, the son she'd borne him. Every night he'd ask his gentlemen of the chamber where his mother was and why she hadn't come to kiss him before he went to sleep. He mostly stayed in bed, except on good days, when he'd have himself carried to a large leather chair in which he'd sit by the fire, a woolen blanket draped across his lap, summer and winter.

This was a tragedy for Harrowsgode. For though

Prince Fredrik was everything you'd want in a king—
sensible, judicious, and wise—he was not permitted
to step into the breach and rule in his father's place.
The law quite clearly stated that a king's position was
absolute so long as he drew breath. That left the Privy
Council in charge, since their official duty was to assist
and advise the king.

The Council, all Magi, held their meetings in the
Celestium, an airy chamber in the central tower of
Harrowsgode Hall. There, all matters concerning the
city were thoughtfully discussed, sometimes for hours,
until consensus was reached and a decision made.

If the Celestium was the city's reasoning mind,
the buzzing hive of government offices below on the
second floor was unquestionably its beating heart, for
here those decisions were put into action.

The heart and mind were linked in the person of
Soren Visenson, the chief counselor of Harrowsgode,
whose title was Great Seer. Every morning he went
downstairs to meet with his principal ministers to hear
their reports and pass along the will of the Council.

On this particular day he'd stayed later than usual
due to a meeting with the designers and engineers of a
new citywide hot-water system soon to be up and running. They were just finishing their discussion when
the Minister of Security came rushing in without even

bothering to knock. He was flushed and breathing hard.

"Your Excellency," he said, "please excuse the interruption, but I just received word that strangers have been seen entering the valley. There are five of them: three men and two women. The men are all carrying swords."

A chill fell over the room—for though their city walls were strong and high, their moat deep and wide, and their ramparts always manned with well-trained archers, they'd never wanted, and had never had, an army. They'd counted on magic and mountains to protect them. And now, for the first time in the hundreds of years since they'd settled in the valley, magic and mountains apparently had failed them.

"It could mean nothing, my lord. There aren't enough of them to do us any harm; and they came quite openly, bringing women. That's not what you'd expect from a raiding party."

"You said they were armed."

"Yes, but I'm told that foreigners always carry swords for protection when they travel. Most likely they're commonplace travelers who happened to lose their way."

Soren shook his head. "Impossible. No one finds this place by accident. We need to question them closely and find out how they came here, and why. But disarm them first—and take care how you do it. If you frighten them they'll fight back, and someone might be harmed."

The minister nodded. "I understand. I'll take my strongest men; we'll go in the guise of a welcoming party and explain that we don't allow weapons here. I doubt they'll resist. They have a similar custom in Austlind, I believe—something about a visitor offering his sword to his host to show that he comes in peace."

"Good. Then once they're disarmed, arrest them. I presume there is someplace in the village where criminals can be confined."

"I suppose; I'll ask. But I'll need a warrant to do it."

"I'll write one out now—for their arrest and for their execution. I'm sorry, but it can't be helped. If they leave this valley they'll carry tales, and others are sure to follow. But question them thoroughly first—one at a time would be best, I think—then come and report to me. I'll be here all day."

"Your Excellency," the minister said with obvious discomfort, "such actions require the approval of the Council. And for execution, it has to be unanimous."

"We don't have time for that. I'll explain to the Council later. For now my signature will be sufficient."

"But, Your Excellency, I really can't—"

The Great Seer shot him a look of cold rage. "Then I'll have to find someone who can."

The minister flushed with anger and embarrassment. "I'm sorry, Your Excellency. I only meant—"

Just then they heard the pealing of the bell in the village tower.

"We know, we know," Soren muttered to himself. "Now go and round up your men—unless, of course, you'd rather resign, in which case please do me the favor of sending in your deputy."

"No need of that, my lord."

"I'm glad to hear it. Now go. By the time you're ready, I'll have the warrant."

As the Minister of Security turned to leave, a messenger arrived. He, too, stepped through the open doorway without asking permission to enter. Protocol had fallen by the wayside that day.

"Your Eminence . . . Lord Minister," he said, giving each of them a hasty bow. "The villagers have called up to the ramparts to say that there's been a death. One of our own."

"Not again!" The Great Seer leaned back and gazed at the ceiling, fighting for his composure. "Drowned?"

"No, sire. He survived the plunge, but then he took a shortcut through an enclosure, and a bull was in it. The animal killed the boy, or so it appears."

Soren turned to his minister, who'd been edging toward the door. "How could your men have missed him?" he roared. "Up there on the wall in plain sight, climbing over—"

"Perhaps he did it in the dark of night."

"And no one heard the splash?"

"I . . . it does seem rather unlikely, Your Eminence. Maybe the sound of the wind—"

"Oh, the devil take you, Lord Minister! This was a needless tragedy, and a precious life was lost—all because of your incompetence."

The minister shut his eyes. He'd moved beyond fear and resentment now to complete and hopeless submission. Had the Great Seer asked him to pitch himself out of the window, he would have done it right away.

"I am deeply ashamed," he said.

The Great Seer studied his minister in silence, considering whether the man was too dispirited to perform his duties properly in this moment of great emergency, and if so, whether the deputy was up to the task. He quickly came to the conclusion that a broken horse was a useful and obedient horse, and decided in favor of mercy.

"All right," he said. "We'll discuss it later. For now, you and your men can go out with the coroner. The strangers won't suspect you. It'll give you an advantage."

"Your Eminence," said the messenger. "Lord Minister. Please excuse me, but there's something else. It appears that one of the principal witnesses in the case . . ."

～✂ ✄～

And so the day went, from one appalling development to the next, until crisis was capped by disaster in the form of two letters, one arriving hard on the heels of the other.

The first, hastily written, came from the judge who'd presided over the trial. He wished to inform the Council that Pieter, the barrister for the defense, had taken it upon himself to invite two foreigners into the city, an outrageous breach of Harrowsgode law and custom.

Then they heard the same news a second time, in more measured tones, from the barrister himself.

Pieter explained that the girl in question wasn't really a foreigner but a lost descendant of the Magnus clan. She was, in fact, the granddaughter of William Magnusson, who'd so famously hidden his prodigious gifts in the guise of a simpleton and then when his little charade was up, escaped through the river channel.

The Great Seer nodded as he read this. Pieter had done the right thing—though he shouldn't have made the decision on his own. The girl could have waited in the anteroom till the Council had been consulted.

Then he came to the second paragraph and despair washed over him. He dropped the letter on the table and cradled his head in his hands. Was incompetence spreading through Harrowsgode like the very plague? What in the name of Magnus had the barrister been thinking—letting a foreign lord into the city? It was absolute madness!

He looked up. The room was filled with officials, among them the Deputy Minister of Security, who was standing in while his superior was away in the village.

"I want the barrister Pieter arrested," the Great Seer said, unable to keep the fury out of his voice.

"I'll see to it, Your Excellency, as soon as—"

"Yes, I know. The bloody papers."

"And the foreign gentleman?"

"He's included in the warrant I issued earlier. But don't arrest him yet. We might need to trot him out to reassure the lady till we've brought her safely into the fold. I should have that taken care of by tomorrow."

"And after that?"

"We won't need him anymore."

⚜ 10 ⚜

The Ratcatcher

THE RATCATCHER OF HARROWSGODE, Richard Strange by name, sat in solitary splendor eating his dinner. He enjoyed the small luxuries his salary made possible; and though he regrettably had no lady-wife or friends to join him at table, he dined on quail stuffed with almonds and dates, a selection of fine aged cheeses, rare fruits, white bread, and some pretty little butter cakes he hadn't been able to resist. He ate them off a silver plate and drank his wine from a crystal goblet etched with a floral design and rimmed with gold (a recent purchase, one of a pair).

He'd lingered rather longer than usual over his

meal, it being a warm and lazy afternoon. Now he got up, fetched a silver tray, and carefully set his platter, goblet, knife, and fork upon it, ready to carry them out to the kitchen where—since he was his own servant as well as lord of the manor—he would wash them all himself and put them away.

He was perfectly aware of how comical it was: a ratcatcher putting on airs. He'd discussed it many times with Charley, his ancient and beloved rat terrier. They'd agreed that the incongruity added a layer of delight to the situation.

He'd just set the tray on the kitchen worktable when Charley announced with a frenzied bark that someone was coming up the path. A messenger no doubt, carrying news of suspicious droppings found behind the flour sacks in a bakeshop storeroom. Or perhaps it was merely a rustling in the eaves, a darting rat-shape spied in the shadows at night. Whatever it was, it would mean a trip across town to meet with the client and size up the situation.

But he opened the door to an unfamiliar face, a lad dressed in some kind of livery; the scroll he carried was prettily tied with a rose-colored ribbon. And, Richard noted with widening eyes, there was a shiny new spinner leaning against the tree out front. Not your commonplace summons, then.

"Richard Strange?" said the boy.

"That's me," Richard said, taking the scroll and stepping back into his house.

"Favor of a reply is requested, Master says."

"And who might your master be?"

"Pieter, the barrister."

"All right. I'll give you my answer as soon as I've read it. You can wait in the garden."

"Might I go to the pen there and have a look at your dogs?"

"If you want. But don't go trying to pet 'em lest they think you're a rat and bite your hand off."

The boy stared back in horror.

"That was a joke," Richard said, and shut the door.

He untied the ribbon, spread the scroll out on his table, and studied it with squinty eyes. He was literate, but only just, having left school at the age of nine; and this florid script was nothing at all like his schoolmaster's neat, simple hand. Richard had an eye for beautiful things, but those blasted loops and swirls made it hard to make out the meaning—which was, after all, the point of writing things down: so someone else could read them.

Skipping over the salutation, Richard attacked the words one at a time, moving down through a string of niceties till he reached the heart of the message.

"Oh, crikes!" he muttered, then. "Oh, no! They can't do this to me. They can't!"

He got up, made a circuit of the room, then sat down again, slapping his thigh for emphasis, and returned to the offending words. But they still said the same thing they had before: that Richard was requested—politely instructed was more the tone of it—to play host to some bloody arrogant Westrian lord who had just arrived in the city and who, like lords the world over, would find fault, demand when he should rightly ask, sneer at Richard's hospitality, then forget to say thanks when he left.

By the saints! And here Richard thought he was finished with lords for life!

What in blazes was a nobleman from Westria doing in Harrowsgode anyway? Some mystery lay hidden there, no doubt about it, made all the more mysterious by the barrister having chosen to lodge him with the ratcatcher. It wasn't fitting, not fitting at all, and Lord Worthington was sure to be offended. Was that the point? Had they *meant* to insult him?

At least the man would be unarmed—that was something—as weapons were forbidden in Harrowsgode. A great lord in a mad rage could be a very dangerous animal, inclined to swinging swords about and never mind who got in the way. Richard had hard experience with lords and their moods, and made a mental note to hide the dinner knives.

Well, there was no help for it. He got up from the table and opened the door again. The lad was still on the doorstep, having apparently changed his mind about looking at the dogs.

"Tell your master," Richard said, "that I will offer up my bed to the gentleman. The lord won't be well pleased at being housed with the ratcatcher—but then I suppose your master knows that already."

The boy gaped. "Am I to tell him *that*?"

"No," Richard said. "Just say I'm willing."

He watched as the boy mounted his spinner, pressed down on one of the pedals to start it in motion, then moved slowly forward—wobbling a bit at first, then gaining speed and balance as he continued up the street. How he managed to stay upright on that fantastical contraption was utterly past imagining, but it was a joy to watch him do it.

Richard went back inside and stood in his hall, admiring once again its sturdy construction, its fine proportions, the attention that had been given to small details: the carving on the corbels, the handsome floor, each stone neatly fitted to its neighbor. They did things very well in Harrowsgode, even in the Neargate District. Even for a ratcatcher.

Then he saw it all through Lord Worthington's eyes—the house was small, there were no tapestries, his table would seat only eight—and his pleasure was utterly spoiled.

Muttering curses to himself, Richard went into his sleeping chamber and began to empty the wardrobe of cloaks, boots, doublets, and long woolen gowns, carrying them to the storeroom by the armful. Next he fetched a basket from the kitchen and filled it with the contents of his chest: gloves and hose; linen shirts, a velvet cap, and those satin slippers he'd never had occasion to wear.

Now he stripped the linen from the bed and put on fresh, fluffing the pillows, arranging the coverlet just so, straightening the bed-curtains. Would a small vase holding a rose be too much? Yes, he decided. It would smack of subservience, of eagerness to please, and he was done with that.

He *would* give the floor a quick sweep, though, for pride's sake.

As he worked with the broom, Richard thought back on the two noblemen he'd known best in his life. Both had borne the title of Lord Carnovan of Bergestadt, father and son, one after the other.

Richard had been born on the Bergestadt estate, where his pa served in the lord's kennels, looking after the hunting hounds. As soon as Richard had been old enough, he'd gone to work there as a page, bedding down with the dogs at night, filling their water bowls, changing the straw, and taking them out when they needed to do their business.

Lord Carnovan the father was a big, coarse, impatient, red-faced, shouting sort of man, an accomplished and passionate hunter. He wasted no affection on his lady or his son; he lavished it all on his pure-bred horses and his splendid hunting dogs.

Most days he'd come striding into the stable yard preceded by his booming voice: "Oh, the devil take you, what's-your-name-Matthew; I don't want the *mastiff*! The lyam-hound, you fool! I want the *lymer*!"

Richard had thought him an ogre back then and trembled at the sound of his arrival. But later, after the old man pitched off his courser one day while vaulting over a hedge, and struck his head on a boulder, and was killed, he'd gained a whole new perspective on the matter. Lord Carnovan the father had been what a lord should be: confident, capable, and strong. He had, in a manner of speaking, earned the right to be rude and demanding.

But Lord Carnovan the son was something altogether different. He had not his father's wit, nor his father's skill, nor his father's competence—just his father's title, and the lands and fortune that came with it. Little Lord Peacock was his whispered name. Puffed up with pride and drunk with power, he'd brandished his new estate like a toddling child who'd gotten hold of a sword.

"I am master now," he'd announced that first day, "and it's of no consequence to me how things were done in my father's time. You will do as I say or you shall be sacked. Am I clear?"

He carried a whip; he liked to use it, too.

Richard heaved a sigh and put the broom away. The bedroom was presentable enough, considering the short notice he'd been given. Now he went into the kitchen and set about arranging a light meal on the silver tray—fruit, cheeses, and sliced cold meat—thinking how glad he was he'd bought himself a *pair* of cups in case he actually had a visitor someday. That was one small humiliation averted, at least.

Suddenly his heart filled with rage—that this, of all things, should be forced upon him now when he was so happily settled, that ugly business all behind him. He was so overcome with horrible memories that he dropped onto the kitchen stool, breathing hard.

The Peacock had been uncommonly proud of the fine dogs and horses he'd inherited—though he'd had no hand in breeding, buying, or training them. They were like the heavy gold chain that hung around his neck and the ruby he wore on his thumb—possessions, things that cost a lot of money. He didn't love them.

Within the kennels, where Richard and his pa worked, the dog most valued by the Peacock was the beautiful greyhound Aurora, and Aurora was expecting puppies. When the time came near for her to drop her litter, she was moved into a private room with a fireplace, away from the other dogs, where she could be cared for tenderly night and day until the birth was accomplished and the pups were well out of danger.

Richard's pa had been given the evening shift. Though he wasn't the senior man, he had a natural way with dogs and was well schooled in veterinary physic. Since Richard was coming up in the dog trade, too—he'd been given charge of the ratters and showed great promise—he'd been allowed to stay with his father and learn what he could.

"It'll be tonight," Pa had said to Richard, "or tomorrow morning at the latest. She's turned away from her food all day—and see how moody she is?"

"If I fall asleep, will you wake me?"

"I will, Son. I promise."

"I wouldn't want to miss it."

Everything was ready. There was a large nest for

Aurora filled with fresh straw, a bowl of water nearby. There was a roll of silk thread and a clean, sharp knife—the one to tie off the cord and the other to cut it should Aurora fail to do it with her teeth. Water and linen cloths were ready to wipe the puppies clean, and a brass bell as big as your hand to ring for help should anything go wrong.

Richard was young, and he'd worked all day; it'd been hard to stay awake. So he hadn't heard Aurora's panting, nor her little whimpers. He hadn't seen his father rise up from his chair to go to her. But he *had* heard, through the mist of a dream, a strange, guttural sound, followed by a crash and a moan.

He'd woken then to see his father lying, as still as death, sprawled across the greyhound, crushing her with his body.

Richard hadn't had the breath to scream. He'd just leaped off the bench and run to his pa, pulling him off the stricken greyhound with all the strength he had—though his father was a heavy man and Richard was still small. He'd laid him out on the floor and knelt over him. Pa's face had been red, and his mouth slack—but he breathed; he was still alive. Richard had found the bell then and rung it hard, setting up such a clamor that it should have woken the dead. But it hadn't woken his pa, nor the greyhound, either.

First a groom had come running, then another, and finally the marshal of the stables himself. By the time he got there, two puppies had been saved, cut from Aurora's belly. She'd felt no pain; nor would she ever feel anything again.

Only then had anyone attended to Richard's pa.

"Apoplexy," the marshal had pronounced. "I doubt he'll walk or speak again, if indeed he lives at all." He'd laid a hand on Richard's shoulder. "We'll call a physician, lad; but I wouldn't store up too much hope."

It was nearly morning by then, and someone had decided that they must inform the Peacock. Richard had been kneeling over his father, stroking his hand and whispering encouragement, when the lord had come storming in. He'd seen the dog, her belly sliced open and the three dead puppies. Then he'd turned to the prostrate man lying in the straw by the birthing box.

The circumstances were explained: a horrible tragedy, an accident, unanticipated, and most certainly unintended. Richard remembered looking up at the Peacock, watching the emotions play across his face and realizing with horror that the man was stoking the fire of his rage. Once he had it blazing hot, the Peacock had started swinging his whip at the comatose man—who had loved that dog with a tenderness her owner could never feel, who would not have harmed Aurora or her puppies for the world. It was as though the lord had been taken with a fit, so out of control had he been that morning, striking the unconscious man over and over.

Richard had screamed for him to stop, even tried to grab his arm, at which point the lord had struck him across the face and kicked him to the ground.

They'd buried Richard's pa that afternoon. That evening Richard had packed up his few belongings and such money as his father had saved. Then when all was quiet, he'd slipped into the kennels and stolen his two favorite ratters, a breeding pair.

He'd traveled east all through that night, the ratters trotting happily behind him. Three days later they'd crossed the border into Austlind. There he'd made a life for himself going from town to town, ratting for room and board. Eventually he'd settled in a midsize town where he was so well regarded that folks from miles around would call him to rid their barns of vermin. He'd even been able to buy himself a little house with a yard for his dogs to run in.

It was there that the Voyager from Harrowsgode had found him and made him that offer—with the astonishing salary, and a house besides—that Richard had accepted. He'd become his own man at last, never again to cower before a master.

And now here he was, all those years later, giving house-room to another Peacock, giving up his bed to the man, bringing him food on his precious silver tray—all of which the lord would sneer at because it wasn't good enough. Why, *why* had he not just refused? They could have found someplace else for the man to stay. Lots of people spoke Westrian. The city was chock-full of scholars.

Charley set to barking again and dashed to the door. Richard hauled himself up from the stool, the arrangement still unfinished on the tray, and went reluctantly to open it.

Had the messenger brought him a dancing bear, Richard couldn't have been more surprised. Why, this fellow was just a *lad*, probably not eighteen. And though he was fair of face and manly made, he looked for all the world like the gardener's boy, come hat in hand to ask was there anything more that needed doing just now?

As Lord Worthington came through the doorway, Richard saw him turn to the messenger who'd guided him there and give him a friendly nod. Not a bow, most certainly not a bow, but an acknowledgment that the boy had walked across town on his account and thanks for doing it.

That was one mistake too many. The shy smile had been one thing—unlikely, to be sure, though perhaps he didn't yet realize what a lowly sort of fellow Richard was. But to give the messenger a second thought, let alone a nod and a smile—*that* had been bloody careless.

Why, you precious fool, Richard thought as he shut the door behind Tobias, *you're no more a lord than my Charley is!*

❦ 11 ❧

Tobias

THE MAN WAS APTLY NAMED: Richard Strange. He bowed and scraped as though the king himself had come to stay. "Here is your bedchamber, milord." "Here is a small tray of humble food, milord." Yet he said it all with an edge of—what? Irony? *Malice?*

Probably both, Tobias decided.

It was galling to accept food that was so grudgingly offered. But Master Pieter, for all his attention to ancient history, and maps, and magnifying domes, had neglected to offer them any dinner, and Tobias was famished. So he did eat, though he tried not to seem overeager about it.

The little dog kept sniffing at his boots—he probably caught the scent of horses—and he reached down quite naturally and scratched him behind the ears.

"Come away, Charley," Richard said, scooping up the dog and holding him in his lap. "You mustn't bother the great gentleman."

It was all Tobias could do not to scream—or stalk out of the house, slamming the door behind him. But instead he drew a deep breath and continued to eat while his host watched—as though Tobias were some kind of loathsome but fascinating creature: a large, hairy spider or a slimy water-leech bloated with blood.

Finally Richard leaned forward and posed a question.

"If it wouldn't be too probing to ask, *your lordship*—where lies your estate? I know sommat of Westria, as I was born there."

"It's in the south, on the River Seren. Where in Westria were you born?"

"At Bergestadt, in the north. So your estate, my lord—is it a *large* place? Do a bit of hunting down there?"

"No, not large," Tobias said. "And I've done a little hunting. Not much."

"I see. Lots of dogs in your kennel? I have a particular interest in dogs, as you can imagine."

Tobias set his slice of cheese back on the tray and studied Richard openly. "A small kennel," he said, "on my small estate."

"You could build it up, my lord, buy yourself some purebred stock, get yourself a first-rate huntsman. Money is of no importance, I'm sure, to a great nobleman like you."

Tobias closed his eyes in despair. It was as though the man suspected him of lying and was trying to catch him out. And though he wasn't especially proud by nature, he hated being mocked. So he carefully moved aside the tray and folded his arms on the table.

"You can stop calling me 'my lord,'" he said.

"Ha!" Richard cried, exultant. "I *knew* you weren't a lord the minute I saw you!"

"Then you were mistaken, for I am a lord. And I really do have a rather nice, rather small estate on the bank of the Seren River. But I wasn't born a gentleman, as you rightly suspected. I was given my lands and title by royal decree for doing the king a favor."

"What sort of favor?"

"Saving his life. Before that, I worked in the stable yard."

Richard was grinning now. Not the gardener's boy, but close enough. "So what shall I call you if not 'my lord'?"

"My name is Tobias."

"Well then, Tobias, I've been appallingly rude, and I beg your forgiveness. It had nothing at all to do with you, just a misunderstanding—and an old ghost that haunts my soul sometimes and makes me foolish. Can we start over again? All forgiven, all forgotten?"

"Of course we can."

Tobias looked away, thinking, then turned back to his host again, resolved to speak plainly. "Richard, I'm afraid I may need your help."

"I think you very well might. But I won't know for sure till you tell me your situation—how you came to Harrowsgode and why they let you into the city."

Tobias ran his fingers through his hair, grabbing a clump and giving it a tug. He'd done this since childhood whenever he was nervous or afraid—as he was now. "We were sent to Austlind by the king of Westria to buy a special cup made years ago by my lady's grandfather, William."

"What lady?"

"Her name is Molly, and she likewise served the king and was raised to great estate. She was a scullion before, if you wish to know."

"It doesn't matter in the least," Richard said, solemn now. "So it was just the two of you on this journey?"

"No. We had a knight to protect us as well as a translator, and Molly's lady companion. They're still in the village."

"All right. Go on."

"We went to Faers-Wigan first; that's a crafts town where the grandfather lived in his later years. But when William died, his family having fled to Westria, the entire estate reverted to the crown. There was nothing left for us to find."

"But?"

"William wasn't a native of Faers-Wigan; he was already full-grown when he arrived. Molly learned that he'd come from the far north—"

"—a place called Harrowsgode."

"Yes."

"But how did you manage to find it? Did someone give you directions?"

Tobias gave a little snort. "North. By the sea."

"And yet you found your way across a pathless plain and discovered that clever little cleft in the mountain?"

Tobias picked up a strawberry and nibbled at it thoughtfully. "A raven led us," he said.

"You're joking."

"No."

"And then they invited you into the city, though

it's closed to foreigners. This is all quite fantastical, Tobias."

"All the same, it's true. Molly's one of them, remember. Descended from the Magnus clan by way of her grandfather. They seemed right eager to have her."

"That much I understand. But what about you?"

"Well, Molly and I are . . . um . . . betrothed." He still couldn't say that without blushing. "She refused to come without me."

"And where is she now?"

"Staying with a distant relative, Claus Magnusson. But I don't know where he lives, nor how to contact her; and I'm beginning to be afraid. . . ."

Richard nodded as if in agreement. "Is that all?"

"Yes."

"Well, there's a lot I need to tell you. But bear with me a moment. It grows dark, and my eyes aren't what they used to be."

He set Charley down on the floor and went to the sideboard for a small silver pitcher. He carried it over to one of the peculiar candlesticks that sat on the table. Tobias had noticed them earlier and wondered what they were—for at the top of each one, where candles should have been, was a shallow silver cup; and resting in each cup was a stone. You'd think they were something precious, being displayed like that, yet they looked like common river stones.

Tobias watched as Richard poured a thin stream of clear liquid into each of the cups. In the time it took to draw a breath and let it out again, the stones began to glow, filling the room with a soft, greenish light.

"Coldfire," Richard explained. "Don't know how it works exactly, but it's a great improvement on candles. Safer, you know, less chance of setting yourself and your house on fire."

"I'm amazed."

"They're very advanced, these Harrowsgode folk." He put the pitcher back on the sideboard and returned to his seat. "That's better," he said. "I can see you now."

He sat for a moment, gathering his thoughts.

"I'm afraid that what I'm going to say will be rather hard to hear. And there's a lot to tell."

Tobias nodded, dread creeping over him.

"You'll have noticed how the Harrowsgode folk keep to themselves. But they set a great store on wisdom, and they want the best of everything. So they send a few of their people—they call 'em Voyagers—out into the world to learn about new things and bring back all manner of treasures. They're big on books and maps, but it could be anything, really: seeds for new plants, precious stones, musical instruments, paintings, scientific devices. Ideas, too: ways of doing things that are different from their own."

He paused, rolled his neck, and shook out his shoulders. "I *am* getting to the point."

Tobias waited.

"Sometimes they bring back people, foreigners like me. They want us for our particular skills: the knowledge of how to make fine, hand-knotted carpets, or fluency in a language that the Harrowsgode folk don't know. In my case they wanted my ratting dogs and my knowledge of how to use them.

"There are about thirty of us here. They give us nice houses to live in and pay us handsomely—more money than we need, really, in case you were wondering about my silver tray, and the cups, and whatnot. But we all live here in the Neargate District, and we don't have the freedom of the city. I'm the sole exception since I can't do my work unless I go wherever the rats are."

Richard sat up straighter now and looked Tobias hard in the eye.

"So that's the bargain. In return for wealth and comfort, we commit to spending our lives here, passing on our skills so the Harrowsgode folk will have them when we're gone."

"Are you saying—?"

"Foreigners never leave Harrowsgode. I shall die here, Tobias, and so shall you."

"But why?"

"Because people talk. And if word ever got out about this hidden city with its great, rich silver mine, and its abundant harvests, and its hoard of priceless treasures—all unprotected, you see, for they have no army—well, you can imagine what would happen. And so they rely on secrecy, as they have for hundreds of years."

"But—"

"I'm not finished, Tobias. There's more. You saw how glad they were to have your lady here, especially as she's one of the Magnus clan. Why, that's like—"

"—royalty?"

"That's it. She's very special. So naturally they'll want her to marry one of her own, someone carefully chosen. Not an outsider, Tobias."

He waited.

"That makes you something of a problem, don't you see? What to do with the foreign gentleman the lady has sworn herself to? They'll go about it as they do everything here—with tact and discretion. They'll keep you apart, bring her into their charmed circle, and try to win her over. Then when the moment seems right—"

"I understand, Richard. You don't need to say any more."

"As for the other three—the rest of your party . . ."

"What about them?"

"They'll be the first to go."

Tobias buried his face in his hands and let despair wash over him. For one brief moment he lost hold of the fierce determination that had sustained him all his life—helping him bear the death of his baby brother, then his parents, and finally sweet little Mary; keeping his wits sharp in the midst of a royal slaughter so he could get the prince to safety; and giving him the strength and endurance to battle an army of demons and go on fighting long past the point of exhaustion. Now he just felt hopeless. . . .

"Mind you," Richard said, "I won't say there isn't a way out of this predicament."

Tobias looked up, all attention.

"It's just that at the moment I don't exactly know what it is."

❦ 12 ❧

A Family Dinner

MOLLY STOOD IN THE CENTER of the large, handsome room she'd been given at the Magnussons' house. With bare toes she probed the softness of a downy silk carpet while Ulla, her lady's maid, unlaced the sides of her gown. When it was loose, the girl offered Molly a hand as she stepped out from the circle of russet-colored wool that had dropped to the floor. Ulla folded it carefully over a bench as though it were something fine, then went to work on the buttons that ran down the bodice of her kirtle.

Molly blushed to think of Ulla trying to make her garments presentable again: brushing them, airing them, mending them, scrubbing out the stains. She might be a servant, but it was highly doubtful that she'd ever handled anything so shabby in her life. The clothes had been humble to begin with—they'd dressed as common travelers so as not to attract the attention of thieves—and Molly had been wearing them for many, many days. And for all but one of the past five nights, she'd slept in them out on the ground.

Maybe she should tell the girl to burn the blasted things. She had plenty of money to buy new clothes for the trip back to Westria.

The buttons undone, Ulla helped Molly off with her kirtle and then her shift. As it passed over her head, Molly caught the stench of her own unwashed body. Finally the maid untied the laces of her underdrawers—and there Molly stood: on a silk rug, in an elegant room, completely naked.

She would never get used to it, standing there like a wooden saint while a servant took her clothes off and then put new ones on. She'd much rather have done it for herself, but that wasn't how ladies behaved. So she stayed where she was, arms held away from her scrawny frame, while everything happened again in reverse: on with the fresh underdrawers; then the hose, held in place with garters tied right below the knee; now the clean shift that went on over her head;

then another helping hand as she stepped into her finer kirtle and all the buttons were fastened up the front; and over that her good gown—the one she'd brought to wear in Faers-Wigan, since only people of quality shopped there—which was fastened with a wide belt, buckled in the back. Finally, Ulla knelt at Molly's feet and helped her on with her little satin slippers.

"I've brought you some ribbons for your hair, lady, if you'd like to wear them. They're the same blue as your gown. Would that please you?"

"Very much," Molly said, thinking back to the afternoon of Princess Elinor's wedding.

It seemed ages ago, though it had only been a matter of months. Winifred had done up Molly's hair for the occasion, weaving the ribbons Tobias had given her through the braids as she went. When she had finished, Winifred stepped back to admire the results and declared that Molly was a perfect beauty—and why had Winifred never noticed that before?

People say things like that all the time, just to be kind, without really meaning it. But no one had *ever* said such a thing to Molly before that day. It had made her heart sing with pleasure.

Then, just a few hours after, King Edmund had been slain, along with his mother and the poor princess bride. Molly shivered, remembering the rest:

Tobias carrying the wounded and unconscious prince down the stairs into the storeroom, where a boat was tied at the water gate—and, oh, the blood, and the sheer terror of it, and the fear that Alaric would die . . .

"Lady?"

"I'm all right," she said, and shivered again.

⊰ ⊱

As Molly descended the stairs to the great hall, she was surprised to hear loud voices and boisterous laughter. She'd met Claus and Margit Magnusson earlier in the day; and though they'd greeted her warmly, they'd struck her as the quiet sort, stiff and formal. Apparently she'd misjudged them.

She stopped just outside the door, listening. They were speaking in Austlinder, but she understood most of it.

"Now, Papa," a girl was saying, "you are *absolutely forbidden* to be pompous tonight. We cannot have you boring our guest."

"I am never boring or pompous. I merely offer such insights as I've gained through a lifetime of study, and—"

"See! Exactly!"

"That's enough, Laila." Molly recognized Margit's voice.

"She has a point, Mother," came the voice of a young man. "The lady should be allowed to find wisdom for herself—not have it dumped into her lap like spilled soup."

"Spilled soup! Oh, Lorens, how apt! May I use that in a poem?"

A titter from a younger child.

They sounded like the kind of family Molly had wished for as a child: lively, affectionate, and happy. Then it came to her with a sudden thrill that they really *were* her family. Distant, yes, but the fruit of the same tree.

She peered around the doorway and saw them gathered around the fireplace. Master Claus stood, one hand resting on the shoulder of his younger daughter. The little girl's face, as round and shining as the moon, was framed by a mane of fluffy curls. Margit sat near the fire, busy with some needlework. And behind Margit, leaning on the back of her chair, was a beautiful girl of eighteen or so, with a straight back and large, prominent eyes. She looked as though she was just about to tell a funny story or play some wicked prank. Molly liked her instantly.

A little apart from the rest stood a lad of perhaps twenty-five. He was dressed in a silk robe of deep midnight blue, embroidered all over with silver thread in a pattern of bursting stars. The silver badge on his velvet cap was shaped like a crescent moon.

Rich, beautiful, elegant, and happy—*her* family! Molly took a deep breath and stepped into the room.

"Ah, here she is!" cried Claus in a booming voice. "Welcome, welcome!"

It was only then, as they turned to greet her, that Molly noticed another boy, much the same age as the beauty. He'd been standing in the shadow of his star-clad brother. Even now she couldn't see his face very well.

"Children," Claus said, switching to Westrian for Molly's sake, "may I present your cousin, Lady Marguerite of Barcliffe Manor, the granddaughter of my late uncle, William Magnusson. Come, my dear, we'll take our seats at table"—Claus indicated a chair between the fluffy angel and the younger boy—"and then I'll introduce my little brood."

"Your *brood*!" cried the angel, pretending to be offended. "Are we *poultry* now, Father?"

"You are indeed," Claus said. "But you'll have to wait your turn, my little chick. Oldest first, remember? Marguerite, this magnificent creature to my right is Lorens Magnusson. We called him home especially to meet you; and it's quite a treat for us as well, for we don't get to see him very often anymore. He lives at Harrowsgode Hall and is studying to be a Magus Mästare."

"Papa is very proud," said the beauty.

"As he has every right to be," Claus returned. "And this impertinent young lady is our daughter Laila. She is at the university studying natural philosophy, and she talks of nothing but *chem*icals and *cor*puscles and *car*bonates—" He leaned hard on those explosive *c*'s for comic effect. "And she says *I* am dull!" He said all this with the greatest affection and pride; the beauty took it with a smile.

"Now on your right is Laila's twin, Jakob. And on your left—"

"Father," said the boy, "aren't you going to list *my* accomplishments?"

He had turned to address his father; all Molly could see was his hair, his ear, and the curve of his cheekbone and chin.

"I *am* the family disappointment, after all. Surely that counts for something."

"Oh, spare us, Jakob, please," Claus said.

"But it's true. Every family must have one. Don't you agree, Marguerite?"

He turned as he said this, and Molly stifled a gasp—for it was the boy in her dream! And from the way he locked eyes with her, it was clear that he had recognized her, too.

"Are you all right, my dear?" asked Margit.

"No," Molly said. "I mean yes. Yes."

A hand reached in and set a bowl of soup before her. Molly looked down, then up at Jakob again.

"I'm not at the university with my sister," he went on mechanically. "I failed my exams, you see—quite spectacularly, in fact. So I'm apprenticed to a silversmith. A tradesman in *this* family—only think of it! Papa is so disappointed."

"That's enough," Claus said. "You're making our guest uncomfortable. And do stop staring at her, will you? She'll want to turn around and go straight back to Westria this very night."

The boy sniffed as if that was somehow darkly amusing.

"Jakob!" Margit snapped. "I'm sorry, Marguerite. He's not himself tonight."

"You forgot about me," said the little sprite. "You left me out entirely."

"I was trying to get to you, child, but your brother was insistent upon—"

"Father," said the beauty, "let's move on."

"Indeed. This lovely creature to your left is Sanna, our youngest. She is a first-year scholar."

Sanna knew how to sparkle, and she did so now.

She turned to Molly, eyes wide, and asked with wonder in her voice, "Are you *really* from Westria?"

Molly said she was.

"Ohhhh—what's it like?"

"Well, we don't have as many mountains as you have here. Actually, now that I think of it, there aren't any mountains at all. Just some very big hills."

"What else? Is it very large?"

"About the same size as Austlind."

"And does it have a king?"

"Most certainly."

"Is he old?"

"Not at all! He's younger than Jakob and Laila. His name is Alaric, and he's very, *very* handsome."

"Oh!" Sanna clapped her hands, wild with excitement. "Ours is old. Have you seen him in person, then—the king of Westria?"

"Why, yes, Sanna; I've seen him many times. In fact, I shall tell you something that will amaze you; just the other day we were walking together in his private garden—"

"Alone?"

"Well, there were guards outside, but yes, we were alone. And he took my arm, just like this, and he held me close . . ."

Sanna flopped back in her chair in exaggerated

amazement, rolling her eyes up into her head, her mouth open wide. Then Molly realized that the others had stopped drinking their soup; spoons in hand, they were staring at her—what? Dumbfounded? *Scandalized?*

"In a brotherly sort of way," she added. "Nothing improper. We're just very good friends."

"I have no doubt of it," Margit said, and changed the subject.

As dish after dish came out of the kitchen and then was carried empty away, the conversation rolled cheerfully on, Jakob's outburst and Molly's indiscretion long forgotten. Soon the family drifted back to their accustomed subjects: the university, philosophy, and corpuscles. Even Sanna, who had little to offer on such subjects, made an effort to join in.

Only Jakob and Molly held back. They sat, eating in silence, pretending interest in the discussion. Finally, at a particularly noisy moment when Laila was making everyone laugh, Jakob leaned in and whispered in Molly's ear.

"In the garden," he said. "By the bench, after dinner."

❦ 13 ❧

Jakob

WHAT A FOOL HE'D MADE of himself at dinner. He hadn't pulled a stunt like that in years. True, it had hurt to be discounted so transparently, especially in front of his cousin; but he ought to be used to it by now.

Jakob understood his father very well, better than most sons did. He knew Claus to be a proud man: proud of his clan, his position in society, and the accomplishments of his children. But Jakob also knew that beneath that pride lay a deep well of disappointment—that he, Claus Magnusson, had been granted no gift at all. He was nothing more than a university professor, and not even a great one at that.

There was the root of the family tragedy: Because, of the four children, Jakob should have been the one to fulfill his father's hopes. Instead, he'd been difficult; he'd denied his prodigious gift, pretending to be a slow-wit and setting himself on a path that led to service in a trade. He'd taken the very thing that Claus valued and wanted most in the world—and thrown it away. Of course the man was angry. But if Claus had tried to understand his son, as the son understood the father, he might have found it in his heart to forgive, and gained a measure of peace for himself into the bargain.

Jakob heard the sound of footsteps on gravel and saw a figure moving slowly down the path, feeling her way in the darkness.

He crossed his arms protectively over his chest. He was trembling a little, wondering whether his cousin would be a kindred soul—and certainly Jakob needed one—or a threat to his very life and happiness. Well, he'd know soon enough.

She was waving at him now, with big, wide sweeps of her arm as though hailing a ship at sea. She seemed so young and childish—and that was odd, considering who and what she was. But then she'd been raised common, according to Claus, and had been given no education. That might account for it.

"Jakob?" A loud whisper.

"Over here."

Now she was standing in front of him—such a little thing, all skin and bones and enormous eyes, like some wild creature. Not timid, though. Not timid at all.

"Well, cousin," Jakob said. "Here we are. We don't have a lot of time."

"Then we'd best get right on with it, hadn't we? You've seen me before. In there, just now, you recognized me."

"We recognized each other, Marguerite. It went both ways."

"Yes. I've been seeing you in my dreams this last month and more."

"They were visions, I think."

"All right, visions. You were always dressed in a fawn-colored doublet, embroidered with soft green vines. And the sleeves were some sort of stiff brocade, burgundy and gold, puffy at the shoulder and narrow at the wrist. Do you have a doublet like that?"

"I do—exactly like that."

"Ah." She drew in a deep breath and let it out. "And you were holding a silver goblet up against your chest, like so." She raised her hands to show him, fingers enclosing empty air. "The base is very fancy—some parts gilded, with enamels framed in filigree. But the cup itself is plain."

"I've seen the same goblet," he said, "except it was *you* who held it."

He could hear her slippers shuffling the gravel as she thought about this.

"Listen, Jakob," she said after a while, "I must tell you something. I was sent to Austlind by the king of Westria to find a special cup, of a kind my grandfather used to make. We went to Faers-Wigan, a crafts town to the south, because that's where he lived and practiced his trade. But while we were there I found out that he hadn't been born in Faers-Wigan; he'd come there from someplace else. Yet right from the start, before Alaric even called me back to court, before I'd even *heard* of Harrowsgode, I was dreaming of you. Don't you see? I was *meant* to come here."

"I think you're right."

"And there's something else. The cup we both saw—"

"—is a Loving Cup. And that's what your king is after."

"Yes. It all fits together. I saw you holding the cup because you were meant to make it. And you saw me in your visions—"

"—because I'm supposed to make it for you."

"Oh, Jakob, I'm so glad I found you! There are only two people in the world I completely trust—my friend Tobias and Alaric, the king of Westria. But even they can't understand what it's like to be the way we are. Talking to you feels so natural. It's almost like talking to myself."

And there it was, the answer to his question: a kindred soul.

They were quiet then for a while, aware that something important had just happened, and feeling a little bashful at the intimacy of it.

"Jakob," Molly said at last, breaking the silence. "I want to ask you something. I don't mean to pry, but . . ."

"Go ahead."

"Why are you a silversmith? No, wait—let me ask this in a different way. Why are you *also* a silversmith, like my grandfather was, when both of you might have been—well, what Lorens is, only greater? Where I come from, having visions and knowing the future are seen as marks of the devil. Here it's a sign of greatness. So, why?"

Jakob turned away and studied the rosebushes, trying to decide what to say. That had been the most personal and painful question anyone could have asked. Did he really trust her that much?

"Let's sit down," he finally said, having made up his mind. "It's not going to be a short answer." He took his time, ordering his thoughts, deciding what to tell now and what he could put off till later. Then he took the plunge:

"When I was very small, I was playing with Laila, here in the garden. I had a toy horse, with a real horse-hair mane and tail, and big, button eyes. It was my very favorite thing. So naturally Laila, being devil-ish, took it away from me and ran away—waving it in the air, you know, just to torment me. I ran after her, growing angrier by the minute, until I was positively beside myself with rage and frustration. She was a fast little thing, but I finally caught up with her and grabbed her by the arm . . . and I remember feeling this strange sensation: the heat of my fury just *pouring* out of me, through my hand, and into her body till she screamed and fell to the ground. And she lay there, not breathing, her skin very white. I thought she must be dead—and that I had killed her.

"I couldn't think what to do—I was very young and stupid—so instead of calling for help I just knelt down and touched her cheek, stroked it gently. I was sobbing the whole time because I loved her—I still love her—like nobody else on earth. Then suddenly she gasped and opened her eyes."

"Oh!" Molly said.

"She didn't remember any of it, didn't understand what had happened. She thought she'd just fallen down. And I was glad, because I was sure she'd hate me if she knew. I've told her since, some of it; but back then I had to carry it alone, and the pain of it nearly destroyed me. I took to hiding in dark places and wouldn't let anyone near. I'd go out into the garden sometimes and touch things—caterpillars, beetles—to see if they would die, but they never did.

"Then I started having these visions of another little boy. I saw him playing with a kitten once. He'd ask it questions, and it would answer. Another time I saw him telling his mother that the dustman wouldn't be coming that day because he'd died in the night. And she scolded him, saying he mustn't make up dreadful stories like that. But later it turned out to be true. And once I saw him make the fire burn brighter, just with the wave of his hand.

"I realized then that we were alike, this boy and me. We both had these inexplicable powers. I found it comforting, as you can imagine."

"Yes, I can. I've felt like a freak since I was seven years old. I would have been glad back then to know there were others like me."

"The boy was with me all the time, but he was always a few steps ahead. He became my guide, my model. When he turned himself into a thick-wit at school—took to asking foolish questions and giving the wrong answers—I did the same. I failed my exams, just as he did. And I followed him into the same trade."

"It was my grandfather, wasn't it?"

"Yes. But William was different from me in one important respect: his gift was not merely great—it was extraordinary, such as only comes along once in a hundred years. So if *I* could kill my sister with an angry touch, then bring her back to life with my grief—for William it must have felt like holding lightning in his hands. It frightened him terribly. That's why he kept it hidden. He knew that if he ever learned to *harness* those powers, they might consume him and drive him to do despicable things."

"Oh, Jakob!"

"What?"

"Did you see—in your visions—the whole of his life?"

"No. I saw him dive into the river—over in Neargate, where the canals come together and flow under the walls—and swim underwater for what seemed like hours, through endless darkness; then there was just a hint of light, and he rose up and out of the water and took this deep, gasping breath, floating in the still waters of the moat. And he was wild with joy, thinking, *I'm free! I'm free!* And that was the end of it. After that vision I never saw him again."

"Oh." He could hear the sadness in that single word.

"Tell me."

"I think he was right to be afraid. He never meant to do harm—indeed, he did a lot of good. He made Loving Cups that caused people to love each other. But in doing that he revealed himself and his powers to the world. Someone forced him to use them in a horrible way—they threatened to kill his family if he didn't. So he made a beautiful silver bowl as a baby gift for a prince and filled it with a hundred curses."

Jakob shook his head, refusing to believe it.

"But the prince didn't die as he was supposed to. William was too smart for that. The curses he made were innocent things, like scraped knees and cold porridge. And he put a guardian spirit in the bowl to make sure everything went as planned—a little man, allover silver, and very kind. He was like a little"—she pressed her thumb and forefinger together as if holding a pinch of salt—"a little fragment of my grandfather, all his wisdom and sweetness, dressed up in a silver suit." She smiled, remembering. "My grandfather always tempered the metal with his own blood to make the enchantment work. That made us blood relatives, the Guardian said. So he asked me to call him Uncle."

"You met him—inside the bowl? I don't understand."

"It's a long story. Things didn't go as planned, and he called me for help. When it was over and all the curses were destroyed, his spirit was released. His body melted back into the bowl. Now his spirit is"—she waved a hand at the sky—"*out there* somewhere. I miss him, Jakob. I miss him very much."

The bright tip of a full moon was rising over the eastern mountains. Jakob watched it emerge and grow until it hurt his eyes. He knew she hadn't finished the story. She'd come close, then changed the subject. But he had to know.

"Molly," he said. "What happened when the curses failed?"

She took a deep breath and let it out, then sat in silence for a while. "William was murdered," she said.

He covered his face with his hands and felt tears stinging his eyes. "That breaks my heart," he said. "I always imagined he lived a long and happy life, that he found a girl he fancied, and married her, and spent his days making beautiful things out of silver and gold. . . ."

"He did all that."

"But not for long."

"Long enough. He found kind friends and was a great success at his work—he was the youngest master silversmith in the history of the city's guild. He had a wife and a child he loved. And he died saving their lives."

"I'm glad. It's strange—I never met him, just saw him in my visions, but I loved him very much. He was like my closest friend."

"I understand," she said.

"Marguerite—"

"Molly, please. Marguerite is for strangers."

"All right, Molly. It's my turn to tell you something hard."

"I thought you just did."

"This is different. And I've been putting it off, because . . ." He plucked a leaf from a lilac bush and rolled it in his fingers. He couldn't bring himself to look her in the face. "You came here in search of a Loving Cup, and I'll gladly make you one. But you can't give it to the king of Westria, because you'll never see him again. Like death, this is the undiscovered country from which no traveler returns. I'm sorry, but that's the truth."

"No!" she said.

"Listen to me: I told you I saw you holding the cup, but I didn't say what you were wearing. Molly, you were dressed in the robes of a Magus Mästare, and my visions never lie. That's your future, and the reason you were called here. You possess the Gift of King Magnus, as your grandfather did; and you will spend your life in Harrowsgode Hall, growing your powers and learning—"

She was shaking her head. "That's not true! I just see things sometimes, same as you."

"No. You're altogether different from me. I can sense your power just sitting here beside you. It pours off you like heat from a bonfire. Even my parents know you have the Gift, and they have no powers of perception at all."

"But how could they possibly—even if it were true?"

"Tell me, when you came to our house, how did they welcome you?"

"Like this," she said, holding out her hands. "I thought it was a Harrowsgode greeting."

"Well, it's not. No one touches hands here without consent. For most people it means nothing; but for those with the Gift, it's like water running downstream—their spirit flows out of them, revealing their secrets. To take their hands without permission is like going through their underclothes or reading their private letters. We only touch those we love and trust.

"It's disgusting what my parents did. They were testing you because they sensed you had some of William's fire, and they wanted to be sure. They didn't think you'd know the difference."

"Your mother trembled when she took my hands."

"I'll bet she did. I'm glad. I hope it gives her nightmares."

"Jakob! Marguerite!" They'd finally been missed.

"In a minute, Father!"

"Quick, Jakob—what about Tobias? Will they keep him from leaving, too?"

"Tobias? The friend you mentioned before?"

"Yes. He came with me on the journey."

"And they *let him into Harrowsgode*?" He was astonished.

"I lied and said we were betrothed. I refused to come without him."

"Oh, Molly!" He shook his head. "No, they will *not* let him leave."

That was the least of it, Jakob suspected, but he wouldn't say any more. He'd heaped enough grief on her already, and there was nothing she could do to help her friend.

"Come *inside*!" Claus called again.

"We have to go, Molly. We'll talk again tomorrow."

"All right. But promise you'll make me the cup, and as quickly as you can. I'll figure out the rest. Will you do that for me, please?"

"Of course I will. But it won't change a thing."

"They can't force me to stay here. I won't let them."

"Oh, little cousin, you have *no idea* who you're dealing with."

"Really, Jakob?" She raised her chin with such childish defiance, it almost made him laugh. "Well, neither do *they*!"

❧ 14 ❧

Watching

HE ARRIVED AT the house before dawn. Lights were already glowing in some of the windows—servants, most likely, making preparations for the day ahead. At sunup the porter came out to sweep the steps, and not long after that a servant left, a basket on her arm. When she returned, the basket was so full she needed both hands to carry it. After that nothing much happened for a while.

Then Claus Magnusson came out with his two daughters. The younger one gripped her father's hand, skipping and bouncing along as they made their way down the street. The older one walked gracefully beside them, her shoulders back, her head held high, and her eyes wide with interest. She reminded him of Molly—they had the same boldness, the same strong spirit. But while the Magnusson girl was confident and serene, Molly was fierce and full of fire.

Well, they'd led very different lives.

He continued to wait.

Mornings came slowly to Harrowsgode, the mountains and tall buildings casting long, cool shadows till the sun was well up in the sky. But by midday the cobbles would be shimmering with heat, and warm currents of air would begin to rise, the ones that lifted his wings and allowed him to soar so effortlessly through the sky.

But not quite yet. The River District was deep in shadow still.

At last something unexpected: a man was approaching the house. He had gray hair and wore academic robes. The raven felt sure that he'd come to visit Molly. A tutor perhaps?

He'd been avoiding the windowsills, which were narrow for a bird of his size, but he needed to hear what the man said. Clapping the air with his great black wings, he rose and circled once, marking a spot on a sill to the right of the entry door, calculating the angle and speed of his descent, then sliding in with a little sideways hop so that he stood pressed close against the window glass. It wasn't comfortable, but he was steady.

The man looked up for a moment, startled by the sound of wings; then he looked down again as the door opened.

"Dr. Larsson to see the lady Marguerite," he said.

The porter bowed and ushered the man in.

❦ 15 ❧

A Little Outing

THE TUTOR, GEROLD LARSSON, was older than she'd expected, and more distinguished in appearance. He looked as if he ought to be teaching at the university, not giving private lessons to someone like Molly.

"Dr. Magnusson tells me that you were never taught your letters," he said. "Can this possibly be true?"

"Yes," she said as if it were a matter of pride. "I was taught nothing at all."

"Then we shall have some catching up to do." He said this with relish, as if helping ignorant girls catch up was the thing he liked most in the world.

"I'd rather you taught me Austlinder. I have great need of speaking and no need whatsoever for reading and writing."

"I think you'll find, once we get started, that knowing how to read and write is surprisingly useful. But we will do both, never fear."

There was a thump and rustling at the window just then, and both of them turned to see a raven clinging precariously to the narrow ledge.

"Shoo!" Dr. Larsson shouted, clapping his hands.

With a flutter of wings, the bird disappeared from sight.

"Why did you *do* that?"

He seemed surprised that she should ask. "Birds are filthy creatures," he said as if stating the obvious. "They leave their droppings on the window ledges and down the sides of the house."

She went over to the window and looked down into the garden, searching for any sign of the raven. At last she heard a froglike *croooawk*—and there he was, half hidden in a lilac bush.

"I like ravens," she said without turning around. "And they're not filthy."

"I'm sorry, Marguerite. I didn't mean to offend."

"They're beautiful birds."

"I suppose they are."

"Stephen says they're very intelligent."

"Yes, I've heard that too."

"They court by dancing side by side with their sweethearts in the air. And they mate for life."

"Well, once you've learned to read, you can study books on natural philosophy and learn all there is to know about ravens."

She finally turned away from the window and found him waiting with a gentle smile.

"Excuse me, my dear, but I'd be very grateful if you'd take a seat. Courtesy requires that I remain standing as long as a lady does, and I have very troublesome knees."

"Oh," she said, "I didn't know."

She walked around the little desk and plopped herself down behind it, then waited while Dr. Larsson lowered himself cautiously into a chair. He massaged his knees for a minute, then looked up at Molly and thanked her.

"Now, I believe there's no better place to start than at the beginning—with the letters of the alphabet. I've asked for our meal to be brought in on a tray at twelve-bells. After that we might move on to a bit of language study, using the skills—"

Only now did Molly understand that he planned to stay all day. And no doubt he'd be back again tomorrow and the day after that, leaving her no time to find Tobias and work out a plan or to roam about Harrowsgode searching for a way to escape.

"Master Tutor," she said, interrupting his flow of words, "I really don't think I could learn anything at all today. I've been traveling for a long time and didn't sleep well last night. I'm bone-tired, and my wits are like curdled cream. Maybe you could come back later—next week, perhaps."

"I quite understand. But let me make an alternative proposal. Suppose we put off your studies for today and go on a little outing instead? There are many things in Harrowsgode that will amaze you, but there's one particular sight that stands above the rest and is positively not to be missed: the Great Hall of Treasures. It's not far from here, and we needn't stay long—though once you get there and see it, you may want to."

"What is it—the Great Hall of Treasures?"

"Exactly what the name implies: a beautiful building with priceless treasures on display. Anyone in Harrowsgode may go there. You don't even have to pay."

"What sort of treasures?"

"Every kind you can possibly imagine—and countless more you cannot. In my opinion, the library is the greatest treasure of all, but that will not interest you just yet. We'll peek in so you can say you've seen it, then move on to the treasures.

"The library is in the center of the building and is very large. The treasure-house wraps around it on all four sides. There are rooms dedicated to paintings from all over the world, and one room filled with marble sculptures. There are works in silver and gold, artifacts from ancient times, new inventions, musical instruments, native costumes from distant lands, tapestries, and curiosities from every age and corner of the world. I promise you will be astonished."

"I've never seen anything like that."

"Nor has anyone else who hasn't been to Harrowsgode. What do you say? Would you like to go?"

As she stood gazing up at the building, Molly realized that she'd seen it before. It was when they'd just come out of the narrow canyon and were standing on the rim, looking down at Harrowsgode. It was the city's most distinctive feature, so grand and imposing she'd thought at first it must be a cathedral, though it didn't really look like one. Enormous at the base, it rose story by story, each level smaller than the one below: a sort of giant's staircase capped by five domed towers.

Leading to the entrance was a broad staircase, which they now began to climb.

Dr. Larsson asked if she'd lend him her arm, as she was young and strong and he was old, with troublesome knees. He held it firmly, just as Alaric had, but the experience was altogether different. This was not the intimate thrill of touching the king of Westria; she felt a tingling in her arm rather like the sensation of clasping hands with Claus and Margit, only very much stronger. She didn't think he'd done it on purpose, as her relatives had—but surely he must feel it. And if what Jakob had told her was true, he must even now be reading the secrets of her heart. Molly turned to look at him, but the only expression she saw on his face was the occasional wince at the pain from climbing the stairs.

"Going down is even worse," he said as if reading her mind. "They really should build a ramp, maybe with some sort of pulley system to haul pathetic old fellows like me up and down the stairway." He gave her a wan smile. "I think I'll write a note to the Council suggesting it."

At last they reached the landing and Dr. Larsson released her arm. They waited a moment while he caught his breath, then he gave her a quick little nod.

"Shall we go in?" he said.

Large buildings, in her experience, were usually dark. But the entrance to the Great Hall of Treasures was astonishingly bright. And looking up, she saw why. The stout walls that held up the enormous structure were straight ahead of her. The entry hall, and the corridors that extended beyond it on either side, wrapping all around the building, were simply an elaborate porch. Since nothing rested on top of it, the ceiling could safely hold countless skylights, as well as a string of small, angled windows placed where the wall met the ceiling on the outer side. She'd never seen anything like it. And all that glass—it must have cost an absolute fortune!

Dr. Larsson had gone to speak with one of the officials, who wrote something on a small slip of paper and handed it to him. Now he returned. "A pass for the library," he explained. "We'll just take a *very* quick look, I promise. But you cannot come here and miss the finest thing in all of Harrowsgode, perhaps even the world—the wisdom of every land, and every age, gathered in a single place." He said this with such high emotion that Molly almost laughed.

"Just wait," he said. "You'll see."

The library door was as stout as a castle gate and made of dark, gleaming wood, reinforced by masses of astonishing ironwork: cunningly wrought vines curling into spirals, sprouting leaves and delicate whorls touched up here and there with spots of gold.

A guard kept watch beside it. And even though he'd seen his fellow official write out their pass, he made Dr. Larsson show it anyway.

"There was a library like this in ancient times," he said as the guard was pulling out his keys to unlock the door. "Nearly two thousand years ago. It had the finest collection of manuscripts in the world. The greatest minds of the age flocked there to give lectures, and read, and discuss what they had learned. It is said that carved upon the walls was an inscription: 'This is the place that cures the soul.'"

The guard had the door open now and was waiting for them to walk through. Once they were inside, he shut and locked the door behind them. Molly was just wondering why they were so protective of a room full of books when anyone might walk in and look at the treasures—but then she looked around and understood.

The place was immense, supported by thousands of stone pillars, each as broad and high as the oldest tree that ever grew. Running along both sides of these rows of columns, as far as the eye could see, were bookshelves, so tall that ladders had been provided for reaching the upper shelves.

This was no dreary tomb of dusty books. It was alive, like a hive of bees, humming with the soft voices and quiet footsteps of scholars. They sat at tables, books laid out before them, talking with one another. They wandered through the stacks and climbed the ladders.

Against her will, Molly felt the tremendous power of the place: all the knowledge of the world collected in that very room, and all those scholars scurrying about, drinking the knowledge in as bees suck nectar.

The place that cures the soul.

"I want to show you something of special interest," Dr. Larsson said, guiding her past more shelves holding an inconceivable number of books until they finally reached the heart of the library. Here was a great stone box, a room within the room, its marble-clad walls rising to the ceiling on all four sides. High above the level of their heads the box had barred, unglazed windows, probably to let in light and air.

"This is the sanctum sanctorum," he said, showing his slip of paper to the guard at the door, who was not so fastidious as the first one had been. He merely glanced at the pass before fishing out his key. Once he'd unlocked the door, though, he followed them inside and was joined a moment later by a second guard.

"What do you keep in here?" she asked. "The crown jewels?"

"Oh, dear, no. Those are on display in the Hall of Treasures. The documents in *here*"—he indicated the rows of locked cabinets—"are of *much* higher value. They're truly priceless, irreplaceable, the rarest of the rare." Then, to the first guard, "The Pinakes of Callimachus, please."

The man unlocked one of the cabinets—there were no open shelves here—and took out a scroll. He handed it to Dr. Larsson, who carried it to a small, round table where light-stones were already glowing. He unfurled it for Molly to see.

"This is a copy. The original is also here in this room, but we never handle it. Old papyrus scrolls are extremely delicate."

Molly nodded.

"Remember the famous library I was just telling you about? Well, this is a list of all the books it contained. If you were an ancient scholar and you wanted to read a certain work by a particular author, you could look it up on the list to see where it was kept. It's an extraordinary document, the very first of its kind."

"What happened to it?" Molly asked, staring down at the tiny writing, the unfamiliar letters. "The library, I mean. Is it still there?"

Dr. Larsson straightened, allowing the scroll to wind itself up again, and said with a strange, fierce dignity, "There was a war. It burned. Everything was destroyed."

"Oh," she said. "That's very sad."

"'Sad' is too small a word to describe such a terrible loss."

"But why didn't this burn up?" She pointed to the scroll on the table.

"The Pinakes was in constant use. There were many copies, widely distributed. A few of them survived."

He returned the scroll to the cabinet, then nodded to the guard, who nodded back. She thought they were about to leave. But the guard, having finished locking the cabinet, now crossed the little room and opened yet another door. She hadn't noticed it till now since it was small and matched the cabinets around it. A quick glance told her that the space in which they stood wasn't square. On the other side of that wall there must be yet *another* room, holding the rarest treasures of them all. She looked up at her tutor, brows raised in question.

"You shall see," he said, ushering her through the door.

It opened—how unexpected!—onto a spiral staircase.

She heard the turn of a lock and looked behind her. Both guards had entered and were standing with their backs to the door.

"You will forgive me one day," Dr. Larsson said. "I'm sorry. But we can no more afford to lose you than we could these precious scrolls."

"I don't understand." She looked up the stairway lit from above by a warm golden light. "What *is* this place?"

"Why, didn't you know? It's Harrowsgode Hall."

❦ 16 ❧

A Plan

RICHARD LEANED HIS RAT-STAFF against the wall and took off his official cloak. "Bad news, I'm afraid," he said. "The barrister's been arrested."

Tobias groaned. "It's because of me, isn't it? Because he let me into the city."

"Master Pieter made his own decision. It wasn't your idea. And before you fall all over yourself with remorse, consider the spot he's put you in. He'll spend a couple of months in prison till the Council gets over its annoyance, but they won't spill a drop of his precious blood. He's one of their own, and from the highest class. You, on the other hand . . ."

"I know, Richard. You've made that point already, and there's nothing wrong with my memory."

"Then you understand that we can't just have you sitting here waiting for the Watch to pick you up. We need a plan, and we need it bloody quick."

"I was already thinking along those lines while you were away."

"Oh? And did you come up with anything?"

"Not exactly. But let me ask you this—as a foreigner living in Neargate, are you permitted to send personal letters to people in the town? By messenger, I mean."

"Yes. Messengers come and go from here all the time. It's how my clients contact me and how I set up meetings."

"Could you send one to the home of Claus Magnusson, even though we don't know his address?"

"The messenger would know where to take it. But can your lady read?"

"No, but she could get someone to read it to her, someone she trusts."

"Well, I don't much like it; I'll be honest with you, Tobias. There are lots of things that could go wrong. But let's just say for the sake of argument that we did compose such a letter. What would be the gist of it?"

"That she's in danger. That she won't be allowed to

leave. That she should forget about the cup and escape if she can. That Master Pieter has been arrested. I'm not sure I should tell her the other bit . . ."

"About the Council probably wanting you dead?"

"It would only upset her."

"It might, yes."

"Then I'd set up a meeting somewhere dark and quiet, and hide there till she comes. Molly's clever. She'll manage to get out of the house. Then we can work out a plan together."

Richard grinned. "It's a beginning. And as it happens, I know a score of dark and quiet places."

Tobias gave him a questioning look.

"That's where the rats live."

❦ 17 ❧

An Amazing Stroke of Luck

It was perfect flying weather.

He floated effortlessly in the sky, held aloft by a cushion of warm air rising from the cobbles and slate on the streets and rooftops below. He had no need to beat his wings—just a delicate movement of the feathers now and then, that's all that was required, and slight adjustments to the angle of his widespread tail.

He hadn't chosen this body any more than a human child decides whether it will be born in a cottage or a castle. He might have stayed as he was—a disembodied spirit—after the spell was broken and his obligations were fulfilled. But he'd formed deep attachments during that time, and even a spirit hungers for love. So he'd willed himself another life, and his wish had been granted.

He'd laughed—well, actually he'd gone *kraaaaa*—when he saw what he'd become. How darkly amusing! Weren't ravens said to be the ghosts of murdered people or the souls of the damned?

It had taken some getting used to. His raven-body craved the most disgusting things: dead mice, maggots, beetles. But his vision was sharp and his hearing keen; and best of all, he could fly. He could go wherever he wanted, the world spread out below him—what a blessing after the life of seclusion he'd endured for so many years!

Now he'd even chosen a mate. They'd been courting since the spring, flying together, dancing through the air, dipping and rising in perfect unison. When he returned—*if* he returned—they'd find their own little spot of land. He'd defend it, and together they'd raise their young, feeding them and keeping them safe till they were fledged and ready to go out on their own.

But that would have to wait until this final task was done. For now he was just one of the countless birds that circled Harrowsgode Hall. Rooks in particular congregated there, but so did jackdaws, ravens, and crows.

He'd been watching the entrance for a long time—since Molly had first gone in—and she still had not come out. This troubled him, because the man—the one who'd driven him off the ledge and had later escorted Molly to Harrowsgode Hall—had left within an hour of their arrival. Why would he do that? What did it mean? The raven was sure he hadn't missed her.

He continued his vigil till the building was shut for the night and the people who worked there had gone home for their dinners. Disheartened, he left Harrowsgode Hall and flew back to the Magnussons' house.

At least he knew where her bedroom was. He'd found it that morning. After the tutor had so rudely shooed him away, he'd circled the house a few more times. In one of the rooms, where a servant was making the bed, he'd spotted something familiar: Molly's comical straw hat perched on top of the wardrobe.

He returned there now and was preparing himself for a tricky landing when he saw that the window was open. He perched on the sill and looked inside.

The room was dark; the maid hadn't attended to the light-stone yet, which was surprising in a household like that. You'd expect the staff to be highly trained and quick to . . . *what was that?*

He stuck out his head and blinked. Over in the

shadows, blending in with the carpet and difficult to see—if you weren't a sharp-eyed raven—was a bit of dark blue ribbon. He stared at it for a moment, tilting his head thoughtfully. Then he had a brilliant idea.

He could see Tobias inside the house. He was seated across a table from an older man with a large nose, presumably the ratcatcher. Their heads were together, studying something. The raven tapped on the window glass.

Tobias looked up, squinted, then looked down again.

The raven signaled a second time: *tap-tap-tap-tap-tap-tap.*

The little dog that rested at their feet jumped up and started barking. The ratcatcher turned in alarm.

"It's just a raven," Tobias said, going over to have a look.

"Then leave it be," the host said. "Stop it, Charley! Come here!"

But Tobias ignored him. He leaned down and stared through the window.

"Richard, hold the dog. I'm going outside."

The raven flew down from the windowsill and waited. Tobias came out, and for a moment he just stood there staring. Then the raven hopped forward, dropped the ribbon, and hopped back.

Tobias picked it up.

"This is Molly's," he said as if speaking to himself. Then he stared at the raven some more.

Oh, come on, Tobias. You can figure it out! He nodded and made another little hop. *Please, don't be such a dullard!*

"You brought this to me on purpose."

The raven dipped his head.

"Talking to birds now, are we?" It was the rat-catcher, standing behind Tobias. Inside, behind the closed door, the dog still barked.

"As you see, Richard."

"Should I be concerned—for your sanity, I mean?"

"Not at all." He held up the ribbon; Richard took it.

"Crikes!" he said. "Is this the magical raven that led you here?"

"I'm rather sure it is. Now will you please—?"

"Sorry." Richard stepped back, but he didn't go inside. "I'll let you finish your conversation."

Tobias ignored the remark. "Did Molly send this to me?" he asked.

The raven thought quickly. The answer was *Not really*. But he dipped his head anyway to get things started.

"Do you know who I am?"

Dip.

"Am I Matthew?"

Nothing.

"Am I Stephen?"

Nothing.

"Am I Tobias?"

Dip, dip, hop.

"Crikes!" whispered Richard.

"And do you know where Molly is staying?"

Dip.

Tobias turned to Richard, then back to the raven. "If I asked you to take her a message, could you do it?"

Dip, dip.

"Will you wait till we're ready?"

Dip.

Tobias stood and turned to Richard. "What do you think?"

"I think it's an amazing stroke of luck, and we should go finish that letter right now."

❦ 18 ❧

Dusk at the Magnussons' House

ONCE AGAIN THE RAVEN stood on the window ledge, peering into Molly's chamber. Tied carefully around one of his legs was a slender strip of paper—the message from Tobias. He'd come to deliver it, but the room was still dark and empty. She must be at dinner, then. He'd just have to wait.

After a while the door opened and the servant came in, carrying a small silver pitcher. She went to the light-stone on the bedside table and poured a slow stream of coldfire over it; the room was now filled with a strange, greenish light.

The maid went over to the wardrobe and took out

Molly's blue gown. She laid it on the bed and began to fold it with care. Then she picked up the traveling bag, opened it wide, and packed the gown away. In the same methodical manner she folded and packed the kirtle, shift, underlinen, garters, and stockings. Finally, she went back for the satin slippers and tucked them in at the sides.

For a moment the girl stopped and leaned against the wardrobe, her hand over her mouth. The raven saw that her cheeks were wet with tears. But she didn't rest there long; she sucked in a deep breath and went back to her work, gathering Molly's few personal items from the nightstand—her comb, some hairpins, the small leather box that held her earrings—and setting them on top of the other things in the bag. At last she closed and fastened it, reached up for the straw hat, and set everything down outside the door.

Was Molly going somewhere?

Now the girl was folding back the coverlet, exactly in half, smoothing out any wrinkles. She folded it in half again, and again, till it formed a neat strip at the foot of the bed. Then she removed the linens from the bed and set them outside the door on the floor beside Molly's bag.

The raven felt the feathers rise all over his body. How had he been so slow to understand? The maid was closing up the room! Something had happened to Molly.

The girl noticed him then. She wiped her eyes and went over to open the window.

"Be that a message for my lady?" she asked, pointing to the strip of paper he carried.

The raven nodded his head.

"I'm sorry. She's not here. Nor will she be returning."

The raven cocked his head, and she seemed to understand.

"She's gone to Harrowsgode Hall, that's what Master said. I don't know where exactly, and it's a great, large place. But I think you can find her; she'll have a window, wherever she be." The girl smiled then. "I'm glad she has a little friend. She touched my heart when she were here, even such a very short time."

And then, softly, "I'm sorry, but I have to close the window now."

Downstairs, the family was at dinner. Claus and Margit had been doing their best to warm the chill in the air, but they had not been successful. Laila was solemn and glum, speaking only when addressed and in as few words as she could manage without being rude. Even the subject of corpuscles couldn't draw her out. Jakob wouldn't speak at all. And little Sanna, no longer sparkling, had turned as fierce and tenacious as a bulldog.

"But *why*?" she kept wailing, refusing to be hushed or even to lower her voice. The servants had long since been told to leave the room.

"Because she must learn," Claus said. He was repeating himself, but then Sanna kept repeating herself too. "She's not had your advantages. She's almost grown, yet she cannot so much as read or write. And she's one of *us*, Sanna, with a special gift!"

"But why couldn't she stay here and go to school?"

"She's too old. Would *you* like to go to school with crawling infants?"

"She could have a tutor."

"And so she will. She'll have the very best tutors to be had, at Harrowsgode Hall."

"Will she see Laurens there?"

"I would imagine. Of course. They'll both be Magi."

"Will she come back and visit?"

"Yes, darling."

Laila snorted.

"Stop that," Claus said. "It's disgusting."

"*You're* disgusting!" Jakob muttered under his breath.

But he hadn't said it softly enough. His father heard, and he looked as though he'd just been slapped. Claus jumped to his feet, red-faced and trembling, not caring that he'd overturned his chair. Eyes fierce with anger, he lunged toward Jakob, his hand raised to strike.

"Papa!" Laila screamed. "Don't!"

Claus froze, and Laila hurried around the table, laying her hands protectively on her twin brother's shoulders.

"Come with me, Jakob," she said, glaring defiance at her father. "You, too, Sanna. We'll go to the kitchen and get some honey cakes like we used to do—remember? Then we'll eat them in the garden and watch the stars come out."

❦ 19 ❧

In the Tower

MOLLY HAD LED A hardscrabble life and was familiar with raw emotions: rage, despair, misery, terror, pain. But she'd never felt them all in the course of a single afternoon. Well, maybe that one time.

Now she lay on her little bed, too spent to move, or weep, or think. She'd passed beyond hopeless; indeed, if the floor were to open up beneath her, sending her plunging to a certain death, she'd welcome it.

All she could manage now was to breathe.

Apparently they'd thought it would be easy. They'd explain the situation in a reasonable manner, and she'd see the wisdom of their words. Then everything would be fine.

They certainly hadn't expected her to fight.

They'd overcome her eventually (though not before she'd broken the guard's nose and given that arrogant, egotistical, haughty, conceited, patronizing fellow with the beard a good, solid, satisfying kick in the groin). And it'd been worth it too, though afterward they'd tied her to a chair. Twice she'd vomited, and servants had to be called in to clean her up and dress her in fresh clothes. Yet in all that time not one of them had raised a voice—well, no, that wasn't true; the guard and the man with the beard had screamed. But the other three, they'd just talked, and talked, and talked. Sometimes she had screamed just to drown them out. But they had just gone on being logical, explaining, pretending to be kind.

Even now those calm, reasonable voices echoed in her head: Molly had been granted a prodigious gift that, like the very sun that sustains life on earth, was bountiful, and beautiful, and good, a blessing to her people—and a great deal else, all much along the same lines. She would get over her "reluctance" soon, very soon, and discover a happiness and sense of purpose she could never have imagined before.

In time they'd broken her, like a wild creature whose spirit must be tamed so it can spend its life working in the service of a master—except that she was too weary and heartsick just then to serve anyone or do anything except lie there in her little round room on the very top floor of a tower and gaze up at the ceiling.

She heard a tapping and ignored it. If they wanted to come into her room and talk at her some more, they'd bloody well have to open the bloody door themselves, because she was bloody well locked in. And even if she hadn't been, she bloody well wasn't going to move a muscle to help them.

The tapping came again. It wasn't really a knock, she decided, more of a *toc-toc-toc*, like a tree branch rattling against a window. And it wasn't coming from the stairway door but from the other side of the room.

There still remained in her crushed spirit the tiniest spark of curiosity. She made the enormous effort of opening her eyes.

The sound came for the third time: *toc-toc-toc*. Now she made a greater effort still; she turned her head to look at the open window. It was round, like the room, and was covered by an ornamental iron grille—to keep bats and birds from flying in, according to the man who'd escorted her up the stairs to her little prison.

Molly squinted. Something was out there: a dark shape against the failing light. Now it was moving; it made that sound again: *toc-toc-toc-toc*.

A thrill rushed through her then, carrying with it

a burst of energy. She knew what it was: the hollow knocking that ravens made deep in their throats. She pushed herself into a sitting position, then dropped her feet to the floor. The thrill came again, with such a rush this time that she almost couldn't catch her breath.

Oh, please don't leave! her mind was screaming. *Please, stay where you are!*

Now she stood at the open window, and the raven—her raven—slipped his head through a hole in the grillwork. She reached out and stroked it gently.

"Have you come to teach me to fly?" she crooned. "For I would gladly fly from this tower if I could."

The raven gazed at her for a moment, blinked, then pulled his head back out. Then, grabbing hold of the grille with his beak, he lifted one leg, closing his talons into a bird-fist, and threaded it awkwardly through one of the open spaces.

Molly stared dumbly for a moment before noticing the strip of paper that was wrapped around the bird's leg, fastened with a bit of thread. "Oh," she said, scanning the room for a tool, any tool, that might help her break the thread. "Don't move." She'd spotted a comb, the one they'd given her along with the new clothes. Quickly she fetched it and slipped one of its teeth under the thread, tugged until it snapped, then removed the little scroll—at which point the raven pulled his leg back out, let go of the grille with his beak, and disappeared. Outside she heard the flutter of wings, and soon he was back on the sill, rearranging himself.

Molly looked at the paper with dismay. It was just a sea of meaningless letters. "Someone sent this to me?" She asked it rhetorically. She didn't expect the raven to answer. And yet he did—he nodded as any person might: yes.

"Was it Master Pieter?" she tried. The bird turned his head away. She took that for a no.

"Jakob, then? Claus?"

No and no.

"The girls—Laila or Sanna? Ulla, then?"

But the raven continued to stare away into the growing darkness, and she began to wonder if she'd imagined that nod or taken it to mean more than it did. Birds nodded their heads all the time—bobble, bobble, bobble. And though her grandfather conversed with animals, she never had.

The raven rattled the bars with his beak as though urging her to keep on trying. So she asked about Stephen and Mayhew. When he still looked away, she threw up her hands.

"That's it, raven dear. I can't think of anyone else.

Winifred can't write, and neither can Tobias."

Now he was all motion, bobbing his head, tapping the bars, and bobbing his head again.

"Tobias?"

An unmistakable yes.

"Someone wrote it for him, then. Somebody he trusts. And . . . he thinks, he hopes, I also have such a person, like Ulla or Jakob, who will read it to me—which means he doesn't know what happened. He thinks I'm still at the Magnussons'—"

The raven croaked, looked down at the message and up at her again.

"What?"

He danced on the window ledge; she could feel his agitation. But what was he trying to tell her? How she *wished* she could understand!

It came to her suddenly that if she had such a bloody wonderful gift that the Magi had seized and detained her, then perhaps she could use it to save herself.

"Give me a minute," she said, stepping back from the window and shutting her eyes. Then she let herself go, slipping into the unknown depths of her own spirit.

It was like being in a windowless room; and though there was no light, she could sense movement around her. She waited for them to come, whatever they might be. She could feel them all around her, pulsing with energy, like bubbles rising in boiling water. Somehow she knew they were part of her, her own latent powers—waiting for her to reach out and claim them.

Come, she whispered, terrified. *Help me.* The throbbing increased, like a pounding heartbeat. *Come,* she kept saying, *come. I'm ready.*

From far away she could hear the raven's froglike croak—but it was soft, soft, hardly above a whisper. *You must learn to read and develop your powers. And you need to do it quickly.*

"I will," she said as though in a trance. "But please, don't leave me."

I didn't want to leave you before, but I didn't have the power to stay. Now I'm back, and this time I can fly. I will go anywhere you want me to.

She continued to stand there, eyes squeezed shut, clinging to the last wisps of her heightened powers as they threatened to fade away.

Is it possible that you don't recognize me in my beautiful new feathers?

She looked around in the darkness now, beyond the pulsing shapes, where something glowed faintly in the distance. It was the thing she wanted—the understanding, the answer to the riddle. She moved toward it with painful lethargy, as in a dream. And when her way was inexplicably blocked, she reached out, her hands spread wide . . . and then the dam broke; a flood of clarity washed over her. She felt it enter her body like a cleansing breath. It seemed to lift her off her feet, and she was restored, as if waking from a much-needed sleep.

She opened her eyes and looked at the raven again. He cocked his head to the side. And she did—she *did* recognize him, then!

"Oh," she said, tears stinging her eyes.

Say my name.

"Uncle."

Say it again.

"Uncle! Oh, Uncle!"

Yes.

"We'll fight side by side, the way we did before."

I'll do everything in my power. I can carry messages and gather information.

"And comfort me so I won't feel alone."

Yes. But, Molly—you have to do the rest.

She reached through the grille and stroked his wing feathers, thinking. What could she send to Tobias that would tell him where she was?

You can do it. You're the clever one.

"I'm trying." It didn't have to be wonderful, just

something he would recognize.

And finally it came to her.

"Uncle," she said, "you must be patient. This will take a little time."

I am always patient.

"So you are."

She went to her desk, a beautiful piece of carpentry, dark wood inlaid with light, rounded in the back to fit against the wall of the room, curving in front as if to embrace her. On the desktop sat a penholder with several quills, sharpened and ready for use. There was a crystal bottle filled with ink, several sheets of paper, a blotter, and a neat stack of books. This was to be her place of study, then. They'd provided her with everything she'd need.

She tore a thin strip off one of the sheets of paper, small enough to fit around Uncle's leg. Then she opened the bottle of ink and chose a pen. She'd seen people writing before and knew there were tricks to avoiding splatters and inkblots. So she followed their example, not dipping the pen into the bottle too deep and tapping it gently against the rim to release any surplus of ink. Finally, poised to write for the very first time, she looked up at the raven.

How I missed you, Molly!

"Don't distract me, Uncle dear," she said with a

grin, then leaned over and, with fierce concentration, began to draw a circle on one end of the strip. It was not as round as she would have liked, but Tobias would understand. Then inside the circle, side by side, she wrote the only letters she knew: *M* and *W*. It was a crude picture of her necklace. He couldn't possibly mistake who it had come from; it was practically like signing her name.

Now, on the other end of the narrow strip, she drew a little picture: a sort of box, and on top of it another, smaller box, then a third that was smaller still. And on top of all that—she was running out of room—she drew towers. They looked more like beehives, and she only had room for three, but she thought he'd understand. Finally, at the top of one of the towers, she drew a line pointing to a round window.

She was rather enjoying this. In a stab of inspiration, she added a bird, not a very good one, flying through the air. And she was done. Her message said, *This is from Molly, I am in a tower at Harrowsgode Hall, and the raven will help us.* What more, really, was there to say?

When she was done, Uncle repeated his contortions—balancing on one foot, holding on with his beak, slipping claw and leg though the grille. Molly grabbed her linen coif from the floor where she'd flung it when they'd locked her in and tore off one of the ribbons that hung down on either side. Then she delicately wound the paper around the raven's leg and secured it firmly with the ribbon.

"You'll come back?" she said, missing him already.

Your tower shall be my roosting place. You have only to call.

And then he pushed off from the sill, wings spread wide. *Whosh, whosh, whosh* came the sound of his flight—silken, like the rustle of a lady's gown. Out over the city the raven flew, touched by the light of the rising moon, until he was lost in the darkness.

❦ 20 ❧

The Ratcatcher's Apprentice

"TOBIAS," RICHARD SAID, "I don't mean to alarm you any more than you are already, but this is really not a good development."

"Not *good*? She's confined in a tower at Harrowsgode Hall, and you're telling me that's *not good*?"

"For you, lad," Richard said. "I meant for you. I never thought they'd move so quickly. The business with the barrister was troubling, a sign of things to come. But *this*, well, it's an altogether different matter. And though naturally you're brooding about it and feeling hopeless—"

"I'm *not* brooding, Richard," Tobias mumbled into

his hands. "I'm thinking."

"Well, that's good. Glad to hear it. Now if you'll just pick up your head and give me a moment of your attention, I believe you'll find what I have to say worth hearing."

Tobias did, admitting to himself that he *had* been brooding, just a little.

"Now that they've got your lady where they want her, you're of no use to them anymore so we need to move fast, before the Watch shows up and—"

"Richard! You've made that point endlessly. I've fully grasped it. Move on."

"All right, then. Can you swim?"

"Not really. I've bathed in a river. I know that if you beat your hands against the water, it helps you stay afloat."

"Good enough. Now, the walls are high, but the moat is deep and will protect you somewhat from your fall. It's not a sure thing, but people have gone over before and survived. The problem will be the guards. They're always up on the ramparts, day and night, and—"

"Are you suggesting that I leave the city?"

"I'm suggesting that you save your own life."

"I won't do it."

"Why not? Do you really think you can rescue

Molly from a tower at Harrowsgode Hall?"

"No. I think that if I leave her behind and save myself, then my life will not have been worth saving."

"Even if you can't possibly help her?"

"Even then."

"The saints protect us from heroes," Richard muttered. "All right, I'd expected nothing less from you, so it happens that I've thought of something else."

"Good. Tell me."

"I've got a job tonight—a silk merchant over in the Western District has rats in his warehouse. I've been out there these last few days getting things set up. Now I'm ready to start with the trapping. For that I always bring my apprentice along, to help carry the gear, and set the traps, and so on. Tonight that will be you. I've never worked for this client before, so he won't know the difference. Nor will my apprentice, because he only ever learns that I have a job when I summon him to come."

"But what's the point?"

"To get you to a safe hiding place. I've already told the merchant he's to leave the storeroom alone, to not so much as set a foot inside it until I'm finished. I always insist on that; if I don't, they're sure to make a mess of my preparations.

"Now, get off that bench and come with me. We

need to turn you into a credible apprentice, and I think we'd best begin with your hair. It's altogether the wrong color for a Harrowsgode lad. But some ashes and a little goose grease ought to do the trick. And don't look at me like that! This is no time to be vain about your beautiful hair—"

"I'm not!"

"—because you're likely to look a good deal worse before this business is over. Now, I'll lend you my old cloak, and you'll be carrying the traps, and the bag of meal, and the lanterns, and so on. You'll look the part—but curse you for being so tall, Tobias; it's really most inconvenient! When I'm conversing with my client, you'll have to sit on a wall and hunch over. Or better still, hide in the shadows."

"And keep my mouth shut."

"That too. Now, I should catch a good number of rats tonight, which'll keep the merchant content. I'll explain that he has to be patient till I've gotten 'em all, and that will take some time. You'll be safe in the storeroom for a week or more, with me coming and going day and night. I'll bring you food and water, and empty your chamber pot, and bring such news as comes my way. After that we'll just hope I get a new job, and a new hiding place."

Tobias sighed.

"It won't be pleasant, lad, I understand. But unless you have a better idea, it seems you have only two choices: go over the wall or hide in the dark."

"I'm useless either way."

"You'll be even more useless without your head."

"So you keep mentioning. What about you? What'll you say when the Watch comes asking for me?"

"I'll tell 'em lies. I'll say you left on account of great lords not much liking being lodged with ratcatchers. They'll know I'm spinning 'em a story, and they'll try to scare me with threats. But rest assured, they won't do me any harm. They need me to kill their rats—which they believe carry the plague, so it's important to them—and my apprentice isn't near ready to take over. I'll be all right."

"Is that true, Richard, or are you spinning me a story, too?"

"Yes, it is."

"Then slather me with grease and ashes and let's be on our way."

❦ 21 ❧

In the Dark

TOBIAS KNEW AS MUCH about ratcatching as he knew about the art of war—that is to say, absolutely nothing. But it seemed to him, as he surveyed the field of combat in the silk merchant's warehouse and Richard described his tactics in rather painstaking detail, that the two were very much the same—except that this battlefield was small, and dark, and filled with empty crates.

The floor of the storeroom was flagstone, so Richard hadn't been able to dig down to bury his traps. But he'd encountered this problem many times, and like any good commanding officer he had an alternate strategy at hand.

He'd positioned the empty crates to form two walls, one on either side of the rathole, so the creatures would be forced to run between them, along a path of Richard's choosing. Then he'd hauled in dirt and built a ramp that rose to the height of the traps. These he'd buried, one every couple of feet, covering them first with half an inch of dirt, then a pile of sawdust mixed with meal. Over this he'd sprinkled a few drops of aniseed oil to whet their little rodent appetites. Then he'd waited, letting them feed for a few nights, putting out fresh bait every morning, till they'd grown bold and trusting.

Now hostilities had been officially declared; combat was about to begin. Quietly, the lantern shielded so as not to alarm the rats, Richard started near the rathole and worked his way back: setting each trap, arranging fresh piles of meal upon them, then moving on to the next one.

Tobias had been disappointed that Charley couldn't come. But Richard had said no. Charley was old and had suffered a rat-bite two years before. It had gone bad, as rat-bites so often did, and Richard had all but given him up for dead. But he'd survived, brave Charley, and had earned his retirement as a house pet, eating scraps from his master's table.

"You don't want to get bitten by a rat, Tobias," Richard added unnecessarily.

So they'd left Charley at home and brought Constance instead. She was the smallest of the dogs, young and eager to perform the task that she'd been bred and trained to do. Now they waited in the dim light, perched on a crate at the far end of the room, Constance in her master's arms, quivering with excitement.

"Richard," Tobias whispered, "what happens when you leave?"

"You'll go to sleep. Then, come morning, you'll wake and use the chamber pot, then open the little iron box of food we brought and break your fast—"

"You know what I mean."

"Actually, I don't. Waiting is waiting, lad. You pass the time and manage not to get arrested. What else is there?"

"Doing something. Coming up with a plan. Getting Molly out of the tower."

"Perhaps the solitude and the darkness will help you think of something. I find ideas often come to me quite unexpectedly in the night, when I'm restless and can't sleep."

"I hope so. Waiting goes against my nature."

"A man of action, are we?"

"You may laugh, but—"

"Shhhh. Listen."

There was a scrabbling sound, then a nibbling, then a soft metallic *twang* followed by a thump and a snap: the first casualty of war.

Now more rats came, one or two at a time, some skirting the edges of collapsed piles where a fellow rat had just disappeared, continuing down the run to the next pile, or the next, until they stepped on a metal plate and were swallowed by a trap. Tobias found it all mildly disturbing.

Rats, as Richard had pointed out more than once, are intelligent creatures; and after a while they became more guarded. They refused to go near the meal anymore. It was time to wrap things up.

Richard had hung a board, hinged to the wall, directly over the entrance to the rathole. It was held in the raised position by a hook, to which a long string was attached. Now he gave it a tug, yanking out the hook and causing the door to drop. With the rathole blocked, and with no avenue of escape, the creatures began to scatter—out the far end of the run, up the sides of the crates, anywhere their little rat-brains told them might be safe.

Now came the mopping-up operation, Constance's moment of glory. And if the trapping had been disturbing, this was truly disgusting.

When it was over, Richard unshielded the lantern and went about gathering the little corpses and tossing them into a sack. That done, he went from trap to trap, pulling out the live ones and putting them into a cage. In all there were thirty-seven rats.

"An excellent haul for one night," he said. "It should more than satisfy my client. I'll come back in the morning and set it all up again. But for now we both need to get some sleep."

"What'll you do with the rats?"

"Kill 'em, bury 'em. Folks here aren't like the Austlinders, who were always wanting the live ones so they could try their dogs against 'em in the rat-pits. Sometimes I keep a few for training my young ratters—"

Suddenly he stopped speaking. He stood, a cage of cowering rats in one hand, a sack of dead ones in the others, and stared at his boots, mouth open. Tobias followed his gaze but saw nothing unusual. Then Richard set down his burdens, sat on the nearest crate, and smiled.

"Y'see?" he said. "What'd I say just a minute ago about ideas popping into your head? They're like dry tinder; they just need a spark to set them alight. So when you asked, 'What'll you do with the rats?'—why it was just such a spark, don't you know."

"Does that mean you have an idea?"

"Yes, lad, it does. I have a great mountain of an idea."

"Do you plan to tell me what it is?"

"Hold still. Let me enjoy myself."

"It's *that* good?"

"No, it's better."

"Richard!"

"All right, now listen to this. Some years ago I was called to a house in the oldest part of Harrowsgode. The city walls have been extended many times over the years to make room as the city grew. But this, as I said, was the original part. The buildings are old and in poor repair—small doors and windows, you know, in the old style. Now this particular house was a good deal larger and handsomer than the rest. The man who lived there claimed it had once been part of the palace of old King Magnus—which was just a lot of puffery, of course.

"At any rate, the owner called me in about the rats, and I looked around the property, getting the lay of the land. The creatures had set up house all over the place: the kitchen, the storeroom, you name it; but they seemed to be coming and going from a single location, a little shed out back. I cleared away all the tools and whatnot and found a heap of rubbish, so I cleared that away, too—at which point I found their hole. They'd burrowed through the dirt, which is uncommon for rats, so I figured there must be a pipe or a drain down there, or an old sewer line, sommat like that. Naturally, I got to work with a shovel—"

"And what did you find?"

"A tunnel. Well built, too, or it had been once upon a time. It was crumbling in places, and full of mud and rubbish such as rats carry in—and the rats themselves, of course, swarms of 'em."

"What did you do?"

"I walled the whole thing off nice and tight. If they died down there, so be it. The stink wouldn't travel, not through all that dirt and stone."

"And now you're thinking that tunnel might lead under the wall. That it was built in the old days as a means of escape in the event of an attack or a siege."

"Clever lad!"

"Richard, how did my question about your caged rats and what you intended to do with them make you think of that house and that tunnel?"

"Well, you know how a person's mind jumps from one thing to t'other? When you asked that, it reminded me of this ratcatcher I'd heard of once who'd keep such rats as weren't wanted for the pits and hold on to 'em. Then whenever work was slow and he was running short on cash, he'd sneak over to a bakery, say, or an inn, and let the whole lot of 'em out. He'd be guaranteed another job, see? But he got caught at it, and serves him right. Gave all of us a bad name."

"And?"

"Then I thought it might be well to hold on to these once I've shown 'em to the silk merchant. They could be useful in gaining entrance to some place we might need to go, like the Magnussons' house, for example—though there's no point now since your sweetheart isn't there anymore. But it did start me wondering if there were any *other* places that it might be advantageous to get into. And that ancient palace—which now that I think on it may really *have* been part of the palace—just popped right into my head."

"Amazing."

"Isn't it? So, as soon as the client has counted and admired my rats, I think I'll just run on over there and give 'em their freedom."

"And the owner will call you, and we'll open up the tunnel—"

"Yes, Tobias, that's the plan. Ain't it ingenious? As soon as I get the job, I'll move you over there by night, and you can be useful to your heart's content, clearing out rubbish, and reinforcing walls, and seeing how far the thing goes."

"That's marvelous, Richard. I shall do it gladly."

"But?"

"Molly's still in the tower. Have you forgotten?"

"No, I have not. But you're safe, and we may have found a way out of the city. Is that not enough for one night? Can't you take your miracles one at a time?"

"Richard, I shall try."

❦ 22 ❧

The New Magus Mästare

THEY SENT LORENS to fetch Molly in the morning, apparently hoping she'd be more compliant with him than she'd been with the others. He seemed relieved to find her already dressed and seated at her desk, copying words out of a book.

"Lorens!" she said. "Where are your beautiful stars?"

"They only come out at night, cousin. This is my day robe, and here's one for you." Hers was made of fine wool, in a deep garnet color, not blue like his. "Let me help you put it on. Your robe of occasion should be ready by this evening. It had to be altered. They didn't have any that were quite so small."

"Will it have silver stars like yours?"

"No, better—you get golden sunbursts." Then, after a pause, "Are you . . . recovered, Marguerite?"

She barked out a bitter laugh.

"I'm sorry," he said. "I wasn't told till this morning that you were here—or, well, the circumstances under which . . ."

"Never mind. I'm here now. Just tell me what happens next. I'm ready to work as they want me to—though first I'd like something to eat."

"As it happens, I've come to bring you down to the hall to eat with the others if you're willing. If not—"

"I just *said* I was willing, Lorens—to learn *and* to eat. Can't you see I'm ready?"

"I can indeed, cousin. After you?"

⚜

The great hall was dark and gloomy, with a low arched ceiling, small windows, and a glowing brazier in the center. The walls were adorned with frescoes darkened by age and smoke, cracked and peeling in places, hard to see in the dim light.

The hall was furnished with four long tables, two on either side of the brazier, at which the Magi now sat, dressed identically in plain robes of garnet-colored wool. It felt more like a monk's refectory than a nobleman's dining hall—except for the fact that there were women among them.

Molly searched their faces, looking for any that might be familiar from the day before. She spotted only one, the tall man with the irritatingly pleasant voice who'd kept begging her to be calm.

"The room looks ancient," Lorens whispered, "but it's not. It's an exact replica of King Magnus's hall, copied many times over the years, always the same."

"But there's no dais. The king didn't sit at a high table?"

"No. He always dined with his Council of Magi—just as you will, cousin. See the handsome white-haired gentleman at the far end of the table there? That's Soren Visenson, the Great Seer. And notice the empty place on the bench? They've put you right beside him. It's quite an honor."

"Where will you sit?"

"Downstairs, with the other Magi Postuläre. I'm still in training to be a Magus Mästare—sort of like an apprentice. That's why I wear blue and silver while you wear garnet and gold."

She stopped and looked up at him, pointedly touching her robe. "Then why . . . ?"

"You get to wear garnet because you're already a Magus Mästare."

"But how can that be? I just got here yesterday—

kicking and screaming, I might add. And I'm an igno-rant bumpkin, whereas you can read and write, and went to the university—"

"Lower your voice," he whispered. "You were made a Mästare because you have something they value far more than education: the Gift of King Magnus."

"But—"

"Shhhh. Here we are. This is where we part ways."

Molly remained where Lorens left her, watching him walk away, feeling abandoned and utterly over-whelmed. Only when the door had closed and he was gone did she turn around, slide onto the bench, and look up.

She'd expected grim, disapproving faces, at the very least curious stares. But instead she was greeted with smiles and words of welcome. The Great Seer, who said she must call him Soren, not Lord Seer, smiled even more broadly than the others. He introduced her in turn to each of the members of the Council, some of whose names she remembered. Then he made a graceful gesture with his hand, directing her attention to the platters of food, and urged her to take whatever she wanted.

"We follow the custom of King Magnus here," he said. "We help ourselves. Magnus felt that servants at table were a distraction from thoughtful conversation. So, please, go ahead. You must be hungry."

Molly gazed at the feast set out before her—sliced oranges, strawberries bathed in cream, fragrant loaves of white bread fresh from the oven, tubs of butter, three different cheeses, and slices of cold roast pork—and didn't know where to begin. As the bread was closest to hand, she took two large slices and smeared them thickly with butter. Then she spooned an ample portion of berries onto her plate, where cream and crimson juices oozed onto her buttered bread.

"You really must try the oranges," Soren said. "I believe they're uncommon in your country."

"I had them once, at a royal banquet. They came all the way from Cortova."

"Yes, orange trees are tender plants, native to the south, where winters are mild. But we grow them here in great glass houses; they get plenty of sunshine, you see, yet they stay warm in the winter." He reached for the platter of oranges, to pass it. "We have lemon trees too," he added.

Just then his eyes flicked away for a second, and a flash of annoyance crossed his face. Molly followed his glance, curious to know what incoming cloud could have brought such a sudden change in the weather. As soon as she saw that it was Sigrid, she understood.

Sigrid had been the only one of the councilors who hadn't greeted Molly warmly. She'd simply nodded; and there had been such a lack of expression on her great, pale slab of a face, it had put Molly in mind of something dead and frozen, drowned perhaps. Only Sigrid's eyes had been alive; and they'd burned with such a fierce, knowing intelligence that Molly had quickly turned away, half fearing the woman might steal her soul.

But it was something else, something quite unexpected, that had drawn Soren's attention and rattled his composure. Sigrid was smiling. And not the sort of smile one friend gives to another, or even the false kind you put on out of politeness. This was the smile of a poisoner watching her victim take his first bite.

Soren met her gaze and held it as long as he could. Then, with a shudder, he turned back to Molly. But he was trembling now, and it seemed that he might drop the platter of orange slices, so she reached out to take it from him. As she did, their fingers touched, and a jolt ran through her as from an unexpected blow. She struggled to catch her breath, but already the vision was rising before her: the Great Seer, sitting behind a gleaming desk in a beautiful room with tapestries on the walls.

There was no doubt it was Soren—he had the same handsome, angular face, the same aristocratic nose, the same close-cropped silver hair—but in her vision he wasn't smiling and he didn't look pleasant. He was talking to his ministers, and he was angry.

Molly seemed to be floating above the scene, watching everything that happened and hearing every word that was spoken in that room. When the vision finally faded away, she felt fried in the middle, as though she'd been struck by lightning. For a moment she just sat there, blinking stupidly, wondering why there was a broken platter lying on the table with half-moon slices of orange scattered around it, and why everyone was staring at her. Maybe she *had* been struck by lightning.

Then her mind cleared. Sucking in a ragged breath, she swung around to face the Great Seer. "You—" she howled. "You arrested my friends. You signed their death warrant!"

A ripple of silence moved across the room. Soren's face went ashen.

"You even locked up poor Master Pieter, who was so kind to me. And then, just now, you dared to *smile at me*?"

The Great Seer rose, trembling with rage, and looked down at her with the same cold fury she'd seen in her vision.

"Be careful what you say and who you say it to," he said. Then as he turned to leave the room, "I really would be a lot more careful."

❦ 23 ❧

The Gift of King Magnus

AND THEN EVERYONE around her was gone, scattered like sheep in a thunderstorm. Soren had stormed off in one direction, the rest of the Council in another, deep in whispered conversation. Molly remained, alone on the bench, sick with fear and embarrassment.

Then, from behind her, "Lady?"

His voice was soft, hard to hear over the scraping of benches and the scuffling of feet as the other Magi rose and left the hall. He'd had to say it twice: "Lady?"

Molly turned and saw a small, plain man with a kind face. "Excuse me," he said. "My name is Mikel. I've been asked to serve as your teacher."

She was still too dazed to speak.

"Come," he said gently. "They've given us a room downstairs to work in. We'll discuss it there, in private."

"You heard, then—what happened?"

"Yes."

Well, of course, everyone had. Her voice was loud at the best of times, and she'd been shouting.

"Please, lady? They need to clear the tables now."

The room was bright and spacious, equipped with a large desk, two chairs, and shelves filled with scrolls and books. Across from the entrance was another door, which led to a balcony with a view of the northernmost mountains and beyond them, the sea. Mikel opened it, letting in the cool morning air. Then he urged her to sit at the desk and—just as Master Pieter had done two days before—took his place across from her.

"I understand you had a vision," he said.

She nodded.

"Our visions are deeply personal, the gifts of our spirits and meant for us alone. So when you and I are working together, I shall *never* ask what you've seen or experienced. But in this case, as you've already shared it and as it clearly troubled you, I wonder if you'd like to discuss it."

She nodded again.

"Sometimes, especially with those who are young and inexperienced, visions can be unreliable. You might see the thing you fear the most, or something you deeply long for. I don't mean to discount what you saw, but I have to tell you, it's contrary to everything I know about Soren and the people of Harrowsgode."

"What do you mean?"

"Our people abhor bloodshed. We have no murders here, nor any other violent crime. We don't execute people. As for Soren, though I don't know him well, he's been our Great Seer for many years; and he's always held the good of Harrowsgode very close to his heart."

"That may be, and I hope you're right. But, Mikel, I've been having visions since my seventh year. That first time, I was chasing a playmate in a game. I touched him on the shoulder, and suddenly I saw him dead of the plague. Everybody laughed when I screamed and ran away. But the next day it happened exactly as I'd seen it. The neighbors started talking, saying I was a witch, so Father sent me away.

"Then I had a vision of my mother's death, and after that they started coming thick and fast, one after the other. I saw my grandfather murdered. I saw evil people plotting against the royal family. I saw the horrible death of a king. And I saw my cousin Jakob, who lives here in Harrowsgode, before I even knew that I *had* a cousin or that this city existed.

"Mikel—I have never had a vision that didn't turn out to be true. So I can't just dismiss it. I *really believe* that Soren is planning to execute my friends . . . and I don't know what to do!"

She was blinking back tears now.

"I understand," he said. "Let me see what I can find out. The Council is meeting this morning; and while their deliberations are secret, their final decisions are not. They're our elected representatives, after all. We have the right to know what's being done in our name."

"How soon will you know?"

"Not till this evening, I would guess. They have a lot to discuss; they'll probably be at it most of the day. But even if you're right and your vision *was* true, warrants issued without consent of the Council are invalid. Your friends should be safe, for the moment at least."

Molly took a deep breath and let it out. "Good," she said.

"So perhaps while we're waiting for more information, we could pass the time with a few lessons?" It was a dark little joke, and it actually made her laugh.

"Why is everyone so dead set on giving me *lessons*? I've gotten along quite well without them all these years."

"You have a great gift, lady, and it would be a crime to let it lie fallow."

"What—you mean that bloody Gift of King Magnus everyone's always talking about?"

"Yes, the very same."

"I don't even know what it is."

"Would you like me to *tell* you?" Something about the slow, calm way he said this, and the little twitchy half smile at the corners of his lips, made Molly laugh again.

"Yes," she said. "I would."

"Good. To begin, then, all Harrowsgode folk have a touch of the Gift, to a greater or lesser extent. But some, like you, have visions; they can see the future and look into the past. Such people are chosen to be Magi Mästare."

"So *you* have the Gift of Magnus, too? And all those people in the hall?"

"Wait. I'm not finished. Even among the Mästare there are differences. Most are like me: useful and talented, but nothing more. Then there are great ones; they are very powerful and are often elected to the Council. And finally there are the rare few with truly prodigious gifts. Magnus was the first. He saw this valley in a vision, you know, and led his people to it, though he'd never been here before. And when he was old and near death, he rose up from his bed and summoned his powers one last time. He split open the side of the mountain with the force of his mind and caused the very stone within to be changed to silver. It's been a blessing to us ever since, the source of our great wealth.

"Of course that was a special case since it was done by the king himself. But the Magi have done amazing things too. We have harnessed nature so that the rains come only when we want them to, watering our fields in spring and summer, though never so often as to rob the growing crops of sunshine. We never have floods, or droughts, or hailstorms. You will have noticed, I'm sure, how green the fields are. It's done by magic."

"What else?"

"We've kept our city safe from invasion for hundreds of years."

"The stone figures?"

"Yes. That's just a few examples. There are many others."

"Did *you* do any of those things?"

He smiled. "No. Those feats were all done long ago by great sorcerers of the past. We still make use of their enchantments—Master Soren continues directing the rainclouds, for example; but he's just using the same old spells. We're no longer capable of anything that ambitious, and with each generation we grow weaker. No one knows exactly why."

He drummed his fingers on the desk.

"But every now and then someone comes along, quite unexpectedly, who is blessed with the powers of the ancients. *That's* what we call the Gift of King Magnus. Your grandfather had it; and when we lost him, it was a terrible blow. Who could tell how many years would pass before we saw his like again?"

"And you think *I* . . . ?"

"Yes. Claus Magnusson has assured the Council that it was so, and Dr. Larsson confirmed it."

"By grabbing my hands? And taking my arm?"

Mikel sighed. "I'm sorry. That was unspeakable. But they felt it was so important, they had to be sure. We've been waiting a very long time for someone like you—since William left us, never to be seen again. But he carried with him the seed of his greatness, and it's found fertile ground in you, lady: the Gift of King Magnus."

"Well, I'm sorry to disappoint you. I possess no powers at all."

"Surely—"

"*They* possess *me*, Mikel. I can't summon them. I can't make them go away. And I certainly can't make stone turn to silver or summon the rain."

"That's because you're a beginner," he said. "It's the same for everyone. But if you're willing to do the work—and I shall help you—your powers will grow, and you'll learn how to bend them to your will. Right now they're carrying you, like a runaway horse or a ship blown off course in a gale. But soon you'll grab the reins, take the helm—then you will truly possess your great and powerful gift. Don't you see?"

She thought back to the previous night, how she'd forced herself to probe the hidden depths of her spirit—not waiting to receive but reaching out her greedy hands to grasp the thing she wanted. She'd called up the shadow of the bold, relentless, swaggering, ignorant, savage little beast she'd once been, back in the days when she'd roamed the streets, slinging insults at her playmates, wrestling in the mud with the boys, laughing when she got the best of them, picking herself up when they got the best of her, always ready for another go: tough, hard, brash, resilient, joyful little Molly—her own true self.

She *had* grabbed the reins then, taken the helm of just the smallest fragment of that which pulsed within her, yet to be tamed.

"Yes," she said. "I do see."

"Good. Then here is what I propose: we will work in the mornings on reading and writing. In the afternoons we'll do the spirit work: learning to develop your natural gifts. What do you say? Will you give it a try?"

"On one condition."

"And what is that?"

"Please stop calling me 'lady.' I'm Molly to my friends."

{ 24 }

The Tale of the Prince of Chin

"JUST AS A MASON BUILDS a wall," Mikel said, "by piling up stone upon stone, so we make words by putting one letter after the other. But while the mason needs hundreds and hundreds of stones to build the simplest wall, we only need twenty-six letters to write any word in our language."

"I already know how to write most of them," she said. "I copied them out of books up in my room. But I don't know their names—except *W* for *William* and *M* for *Martha.*"

"*M* is also for *Molly,* you know. Look."

Molly, he wrote. "That's you."

She stared at the word, enchanted.

"Now you write it—you'll want to do it several times, till you have it down by heart."

Molly, she wrote. *Molly Molly Molly Molly*

How often had she said, with defiant pride in her own ignorance, "I can't even write my own name!"? What a load of horse flop! Why be proud of that?

Suddenly she understood fully, and for the first time, the power of the written word. It could bridge the gap that separated her from her friends outside the tower. Once she'd learned how to read and write, she could say anything she liked to anyone she wanted, even though they'd locked her up and the others were far away. And they in turn could tell her things: whether they were safe or not, what plans they might be hatching, or simply that they missed her. As long as she had a window—and a raven to carry her letters— Molly would be able to speak to the world.

She threw herself into her lessons with a passion that astonished her teacher; and by midday, when a servant arrived bringing their meals on a tray, she'd mastered all the letters, and the sounds they commonly made, and had moved on to writing easy words.

After they'd finished their bread and mutton stew and the trays had been cleared away, Mikel sketched out his plans for the afternoon. "You've crammed a lot of new things into your head this morning; now you should give them a chance to settle in. Practice a bit in the evening if you like, and we'll start again tomorrow. But there is such a thing as overdoing."

"I'm not tired. I could work all day."

"I have no doubt of that. But if you'll indulge me, I'd like to show you a few things. I believe they'll help you see your task from a broader perspective. Our work this morning was like kneeling down and gazing at a single blade of grass. Now let's stand up and take a look at the whole meadow." When she seemed reluctant, he added, "It's interesting, I promise."

Mikel went to the bookshelf and came back with a scroll. He stood by her chair and unrolled it in front of her—just as Gerold Larsson had shown her the Pinakes of Callimachus before luring her through that little door into the prison of Harrowsgode Hall.

"This is a replica of a manuscript that is more than a thousand years old. It was written by a Gracian scholar in an alphabet that's different from ours. The title of the book is *Geometry*—that's a branch of mathematics—and here is how the word looks in ancient Gracian."

He took her pen and carefully wrote:

Γεωμετρία

Molly stared at it, tilting her head this way and

that. Most of the letters looked strange, but not all of them did. "I see a *t*, and a *p*, and an *i*."

"Yes, very good. Our alphabets are related—distant relatives, you might say."

He put the Gracian scroll away and came back with a different one.

"Now, this comes from the ancient kingdom of Chin," he said. "And I'm sure you can see that it's entirely different—not only from the alphabet you learned this morning, but also from the Gracian writing I just showed you. That's because the Chin don't use an alphabet at all. They write with pictures, a special character for each word. You read it from top to bottom and from right to left, see?"

"A picture for every single word—how could anyone learn them all?"

"Well, it *is* difficult, but not as hard as you'd think. I hesitate to go into it too deeply for fear I'll give you false information. You might want to discuss it with Sigrid; she's an expert on the Chin."

Molly shuddered at the thought. "I'd rather not."

"Well, all right. Let's pretend there's a certain character that means 'building.' If you start with that character and add, say, two strokes on top, it becomes 'palace.' If you leave off the strokes but put a dot in the middle, it means 'cottage.' And so on, for all the different kinds of buildings. Do you see?"

She nodded.

"Now, this book is a history—that means it's a collection of stories about things that really happened. And the title is written—"

"What kind of stories?"

"Mostly about kings and wars, I believe—though I've never actually read the book, not even in translation. Sigrid has, of course, and she's told me a few."

"Do you remember any of them?"

"Yes. There's one about a prince . . ."

She folded her hands and looked up at him expectantly.

"Oh, all right," he said, smiling. "Though I'm no great storyteller, I warn you.

"There was once a prince of Chin who went to war. He was captured in battle and taken prisoner by his enemies." Mikel stopped suddenly, his face flushed with embarrassment. He'd only just realized how inappropriate the story was, considering the parallels to Molly's situation. "Oh!" he said, "I'm sorry."

"Well, I'm not," she said, "but I *will* be if you don't finish. I'll pout and be difficult for the rest of the afternoon."

He managed a wan smile. "Are you sure? I would never want to cause you any more distress than—"

"Just tell the story."

He closed his eyes, sucked in a lung full of air, and launched back into the shockingly inappropriate tale of the prince of Chin.

"The prince was confined in a high place, the Tower of the Golden Phoenix"—another deep breath, followed by a wince—"with no possible means of escape. But he came up with a clever plan. He attached himself to a kite, leaped from the tower, and soared away through the air as birds do, out over the city walls and into the countryside, where he landed safely."

"Now, see—that was a wonderful story! What's a kite?"

"An invention of the Chin people made of sticks and paper, and tethered by a string. You throw it up in the air, and the wind catches it and carries it into the heavens. We have one downstairs, in the Great Hall of Treasures."

"I never got to see the treasures. I was supposed to, but Dr. Larsson brought me here instead."

There seemed no end to Mikel's discomfiture.

"I'm truly sorry," he said. And then, after an apparent struggle, "There are many among us who feel quite ashamed of . . . the way you were treated. It did not become us. Believe me, that's not who we are."

She almost asked if, that being the case, she was

actually free to go; but she already knew the answer, and it wasn't Mikel's fault.

"I'm glad to know that" was all she said. "So what happened next? Is that the end of the story? Or did the prince return to his father, the king, and go on to rule the land of Chin and have more adventures?"

"No."

"Why not?"

"He was captured again and put to death."

"Oh."

"Such a story to tell a young girl!" Mikel muttered, shaking his head in dismay. "I beg you to forget it if you can."

"I will," she said. "It's forgotten already."

It wasn't, of course—not in the least. The tale of the prince and his marvelous escape had lodged itself firmly in her mind. And while she appeared to be listening as Mikel continued with his lesson, she was actually thinking about the kite. If she was going to build one—as she now intended to do—and risk her life on having built it correctly, then she needed to know what they looked like and learn what made them fly. And to do that she'd have to go downstairs to the Hall of Treasures.

"Mikel?" she said, apparently interrupting him in midsentence, or so she judged by his startled expression. "Could I ask you a question?"

"Of course."

"The Hall of Treasures . . ."

"Yes?"

"As I said before, I never got to see it. I was supposed to; that's what I was told. But then I was whisked away instead. So naturally I was very disappointed—"

"Molly?"

"What?"

"Would you like to see the treasures?"

"Yes, I would."

"Then I will see that you do, this very night. And unlike Dr. Larsson, *I* shall keep my promise."

❧ 25 ❧

An Incident in the Celestium

THE FIVE TOWERS OF Harrowsgode Hall varied in style from the rest of the building. They were more ornate and were covered with fanciful carvings; they rose, level by level, in a series of concentric rings, each smaller than the one below, forming a smoothly tapered dome that came to a point at the top.

There was a tower at each of the four corners of the building with a fifth, much broader and taller than the others, in the middle. And near the top of this central tower was a large, handsome room: the Celestium.

On this particular morning, every rook, jackdaw, raven, and crow in Harrowsgode seemed to have gathered there, all of them perched on the very same ring. So it was with some difficulty that Uncle managed to find a place to land, starting a wing-flapping scuffle with a pair of rooks. But they quickly settled down; none of them wanted to miss the show.

The windows of the Celestium were tall and wide, separated by slender columns of stone. The effect was that of a space entirely walled with glass. In the center of this round room was a round table at which thirteen Magi now sat, dressed in their ceremonial caps and robes, the gold embroidery sparkling in the sunlight. They were deep in heated conversation.

"And when exactly had you planned to tell us, Soren?" asked a red-faced Magus. Both his question and his anger were directed at a man with silver hair and the face of an aristocrat.

"As soon as I was able," the man said. He seemed surprisingly calm, considering the fact that everyone in the room was looking daggers at him. "It was a crisis situation. I had serious matters to deal with, and new information was coming in by the minute. There wasn't time to convene the Council, let alone hold a meeting."

"Then you should have called us into your office, or at the very least told us what was happening."

"If I had, Oskar, we'd still be down there talking in

circles, and nothing would have gotten done."

"Well, that would have been a blessing," said another Magus, leaning in closer, jutting out her chin. "Because what you did was illegal. You had no authority to issue those warrants—not on your own, not without approval by the Council."

There was a hum of agreement from others in the room.

"I'm afraid you're mistaken. As Great Seer, I have the authority—indeed the responsibility—to act on my own in times of peril—"

"*Peril?*" Oskar laughed. "From five people—two of them women—who came here to shop for a cup? Is *that* the terrible menace that caused you to throw all law and custom aside and sign, without consulting us, warrants for *execution*? Unbelievable!" He slapped a meaty hand on the table for emphasis, causing several of the Magi to jump.

"It was not a decision lightly made," the Great Seer said, "but I assure you it was the right one. If those foreigners are permitted to leave, they'll carry tales; and sooner or later we'll be invaded. So put these two on the balance scale, members of the Council: the lives of four strangers—foreigners who intruded where they did not belong—against the loss of our city and our whole way of life. Which tips the heaviest?"

"First of all, Soren," said a plain, big-boned woman, "they aren't 'foreigners'—they're people. And the very foundation of our 'way of life'—which you're so eager to protect—is that we never shed human blood. Twice King Magnus walked away from a kingdom he might have ruled—first from his ancestral homeland and then from Budenholme—because he would not fight and kill in order to keep them. What you did yesterday wasn't just some minor breach of protocol. It was a betrayal of everything we are."

The Great Seer leaned back in his chair and cocked his head as though the acrobats had just come in and he expected to be delighted.

"So. We should just let them go back to Westria, is that it? Though maybe before they leave we ought to ask them to swear an oath—you know, promising never to reveal our location, or our wealth, or the curious fact that we don't have an army, that sort of thing. Well, here's a bit of hard truth, Sigrid: people lie. People break their oaths. And I'm not willing to risk everything we've built, and the lives of all our citizens, on the very slim chance that these particular strangers happen to be paragons of virtue."

Sigrid didn't flinch. "I'm well aware of the frailties of human nature. And no, that is not what I propose. I think we should find another, better way, as we have for hundreds of years."

"And what would that be?"

"Enchantment."

They were both standing now, staring at each other as though they were the only two people in the room.

"Got something up your sleeve, Sigrid? Some old charm, long forgotten, just turned up in a dusty corner of the library the other day?"

"I do, Soren—have *something up my sleeve*. I'm glad it amuses you."

"And what sort of charm would this be?"

"Forgetfulness. I've been studying it for over a year, mostly in texts of the Chin. My purpose was to ease the pain of dark remembrance. But with some slight adjustments—"

"Ah. Not quite ready yet."

"I need a little more time, yes—to be sure that it will work."

"What a pity, Sigrid. We don't *have* time."

"Yes, we do. The three in the village will wait for the others, at least for a while."

"And what if they don't? What if they decide that it's been too long, that they ought to go for help—while you're still down in the library tinkering with your little charm?"

She didn't reply, and no one spoke. For a long time

they just stood there, motionless, their eyes locked in a silent exchange of intense and mutual loathing. Then Soren squinted as an animal does—lip raised, canines revealed—just before lunging at your throat.

"I challenge you," Sigrid said.

Soren laughed, and the tension broke. "But that's absurd! No one's done that for a hundred years. Maybe two."

"All the same, it's spelled out quite clearly in the Edicts of the Magi, composed by King Magnus himself."

"You *have* been a busy girl."

"Do you accept?"

"Sigrid, those birds out there are more qualified to be Great Seer than you are. Why, you haven't been on the Council more than six or seven years."

"And you've been on it far too long. You're required to accept my challenge, you know, or refuse and step down. That's in the Edicts, too."

"When this is over," he said, "I shall have you removed from the Council."

"I'm afraid you can't do that. If I defeat you, I become Great Seer; if I fail, we remain as we are. Do you accept my challenge, or will you step down? I'm asking now for the third time. You must say yes or no."

There followed a long pause. The birds outside

leaned in expectantly.

"This is such a waste of precious time."

"Nevertheless."

"All right. I accept your challenge."

"Here it comes," said one of the rooks.

"Are they going to fight? With swords?"

"I don't think so. Wait and see."

The other Magi rose from the table and went to stand against the stairway door. Soren and Sigrid stayed as they were, facing each other across the table.

Slowly the rumbling began, growing deeper and louder till it was painful to hear: an ominous sound, like an avalanche, an earthquake, or the end of the world. Now the room began to fill with mist, and the light streaming in through the windows turned it to golden fire. It grew brighter and brighter, almost blinding to look at—and then it began to pulse.

Uncle drew himself into his feathers as he did in stormy weather, shutting his eyes tight. But this storm penetrated every pore of his being till he feared for his very life. He would have flown away, but he doubted he had the strength. So he remained there, trembling, until suddenly there came a great, loud *whoosh*, as when a great, old tree goes down in a tempest. And then—utter silence.

He blinked. Inside the room, Soren stood as

before, though he trembled; and his handsome face was drained of all of its color. Sigrid had dropped to the floor, where she crouched, arms protectively over her head. And for the longest time no one moved. Finally two of the Magi came forward and helped Sigrid rise.

"Does the Council agree that all was done in accordance with ancient law and that I remain Great Seer?"

Solemnly, the Magi nodded assent.

"Sigrid, this has to be unanimous—or would you like to do that again?"

"I admit defeat," she said. "Your powers are greater than mine."

"So they are."

"But I am still a member of the Council," she said. Her voice was so weak the birds could hardly catch the words. "So I hereby propose that the warrants illegally issued yesterday be declared null and void, that the barrister be released, and that the prisoners in the village stand under no threat of execution. They should be closely watched but given their freedom. I believe, in this case, unanimity is not required."

"I so move," said Oskar.

"All in favor—"

❦ 26 ❦

Hard Things

THE GREAT HALL OF MAGNUS was transformed by night. The green glow of light-stones—in silver stands on every table and along the back wall in little niches—pierced the darkness like a hundred brilliant stars. Heavy damask linen was draped over the tables, and the Magi were dressed in their robes of occasion: garnet silk embroidered with gold. Above the hum of quiet voices, Molly heard the plaintive sound of a lute.

It was early yet. They all stood around talking in little groups, waiting for the others to arrive. Molly went straight to find Mikel.

"It's been arranged," he said. "We'll go down right after dinner."

"Good," she said. "Thanks."

"There won't be time to see everything, but I've drawn up a list of the finest pieces in the collection. And I've asked a few Magi—experts on those particular items—to come with us and say a few words. It should be very nice."

"Have you heard anything about the Council meeting?"

"Yes." He lowered his voice now, so she had to lean in to hear. "You have nothing to worry about. There will be no executions, and Pieter is a free man."

"But what does that mean? That my vision was wrong, and Soren—"

"Shhh."

She dropped to a whisper. "—and Soren never signed those warrants? Or was everything I saw really true, but he later changed his mind?"

"I don't know. It was worded exactly as I told you: there will be no executions, and the barrister is free."

"What about my friends in the village? And what about Tobias? Are *they* free?"

"Who is Tobias?"

"My friend, part of our group. He came into the city with me. Soren said, in my vision, that Tobias was to be watched until I was brought 'safely into the fold,' then treated like the others."

Mikel gave a little shudder of disgust. "Well, there won't be any executions; that much is clear."

Out of the corner of her eye she saw Soren enter the room. He moved with swanlike grace, his head held high, his face radiant.

"Mikel, can't I eat at your table?"

"No," he said. "You'll just make things worse."

"I'll go upstairs then, pretend I'm sick."

"Molly, look at me! This morning you publicly charged that man with grievous crimes. The *Great Seer*, in front of all the Council! Now, until you know for certain that he did any of those things, you'd best keep your tongue and be gracious. He'll do the same, I imagine. Soren's not a man to hold childish grudges."

"I can't."

"Yes, you can. There are times in life when we have to do hard things. This is one of them. So be pleasant—and if you can't manage that, keep quiet." Mikel leaned in so close now, she could feel his breath on her cheek. "You *don't* want Soren for an enemy. Do you understand?"

⚓

Molly slipped into her place at the end of the bench, keeping her eyes down, feeling the heat in her cheeks.

"Well, look at you!" Molly recognized the youthful

voice of Liv, the Magi with the large, handsome eyes. "Your first night to wear the robe of a Magus Mästare! It suits you perfectly, like you were born to wear it. But then I guess you were."

"Congratulations," said the man with the heavy eyebrows whose name she couldn't remember. "The first time is always a great occasion. You should be very proud."

Molly nodded, not yet able to speak.

"I understand you worked with Master Mikel today." Molly felt a jolt go through her. It was Soren's voice. "Were you pleased?"

"I liked him very much," she said, meeting Soren's eyes, surprised to find no anger there.

"We thought it would be a good fit."

"He's very patient and kind."

"So he is. Did you make progress?"

Waiters were bringing in the food now, reaching in to set platters on the table, pouring the wine.

"I did." Then, with a sheepish smile, "I can write my name now. I couldn't before."

She wondered if they would laugh at her or cast little glances of amusement at one another, but they didn't. They seemed genuinely pleased, even Soren.

"Two milestones in a single day," he said. "You've become a Magus and a writer both."

Platters were passed, conversation flowed, and Molly thought with amazement how masterfully it had all been done. No going straight at it with blunt words, her accustomed way. No awkward silence or piercing stares. Just courtesy, warmth, and reassurance, then, "Won't you pass the carrots?"

Was it real, she wondered—or just manners?

✤ 27 ✤

The Hall of Treasures

THEY PROCEEDED DOWN the long, silent corridor like priests in procession. Molly was in the middle—Magi ahead of her, Magi behind—like an effigy of the Virgin being carried through the streets on Lady Day. Each of them held a light-stone in a small silver cup, casting eerie shadows against the floors and walls.

They went first to the gallery of pictures and stopped before a scroll, perhaps ten feet long, which was laid out on a table. It had already been prepared for viewing, a string of light-stones glowing behind it in wrought-iron stands.

The scroll was one single, continuous drawing

of a river and the road that ran beside it. There were many small figures traveling from one village to the next with their oxcarts and horses, their children and dogs. Boats floated on the water; fishermen stood on the shore. And in the trees perched tiny birds.

The Magi stepped back to give Molly space to admire the scroll—all except Sigrid, who came forward to address the group.

"This scroll comes to us from the land of Chin," she began. "It was painted with colored inks on silk—"

Molly leaned down, her nose nearly touching the paper, and studied the pictures, a tapestry of scenes from the everyday life of those long-ago people. There was a man whipping a boy, a woman shopping at an outdoor market, an overturned cart, a young couple kissing, an old man peeing into the river.

"—in the court style, which is marked by a meticulous technique and is noticeably less spontaneous than—"

Molly suddenly wondered whether she was supposed to be looking at the scroll or paying attention to the lecture. Her first instinct, to look at the pictures, had probably been wrong since she was habitually rude. So she stood back up, clasped her hands in front of her, and pretended to be interested as Sigrid continued to speak, woodenly, using lots of big words.

"Please observe the difference between this scroll and the picture that hangs above it."

There followed a weighty pause till Molly noticed that everyone was looking at her. Had that been a question? Was she supposed to say something? Should she be *looking* at the painting that hung above the scroll?

Probably yes to all.

"Um," she said, giving it a quick glance. "The one up there looks more, um, real."

"Yes. That's exactly what the artist was striving to achieve, in accordance with what his culture considered to be the highest purpose of art: to capture reality in the form of ideal beauty.

"But the people of Chin have an altogether different tradition, a concept of art that is based on spontaneous lines, drawn with a brush. They learn it from childhood, since they write their characters, not with a pen as we do, but with brush and ink. They regard beautiful writing to be high art in itself—"

Then it slammed into Molly like a punch in the gut: Sigrid wasn't there to talk about the *kite*! She'd been invited to do what she was doing now: give a boring lecture about a stupid scroll!

Molly hadn't *asked* to see the kite, not specifically. She'd already shown too much interest in the prince of Chin and his escape from the tower. She didn't want to raise any suspicions that she was planning to follow his example. She'd just assumed that since Sigrid was on the list, the kite would be, too.

"—so that every stroke is clearly seen, nothing is hidden, and the artist is revealed. They would never pile one brushstroke on top of another till they all blended together, as this painter has done. It's not in keeping with their sense of beauty."

Molly had stopped listening; she just gazed at the floor, desperate for the lecture to be over. She didn't care about the bloody Chin and their bloody brushes. All she'd ever wanted was—

It was quiet again. She looked up and saw that Sigrid was waiting, with that same flat expression, for Molly to answer—what? Another question?

"That's very interesting," she said, at a total loss.

God's bones, what a tragic waste of the Gift! The girl has the brains of a goat.

Molly gasped, and, without intending to, covered her mouth with her hand. In the brief moment that followed—while she was wondering if anyone had noticed, and hoping they hadn't—she saw that Sigrid's half-closed eyes, which made her look so condescending, had widened, and her mouth was open.

Sigrid knew about "the bloody Chin and their bloody brushes," just as Molly knew that Sigrid thought she had "the brains of a goat."

They were reading each other's thoughts!

"Yes," Sigrid said. "That is extremely interesting." And Molly knew she wasn't referring to the Chin and their sense of beauty.

They were connected somehow, Molly and this dreadful woman—not as friends or kindred spirits, but as the owl and the field mouse are. So what did the mouse do when the owl's great shadow passed across the moonlit meadow? It darted into its hole, that's what.

Where was hers?

The group was moving now, on to the next item on the tour, oblivious of the remarkable exchange that had just taken place.

They stopped before a stone carving of a foreign god. He had the plump cheeks of a baby and too many arms, which made him look like a fat, jolly spider. It was Oskar's turn to stand up front and explain things, none of which Molly heard. She was still puzzling over Sigrid, whose mind had gone silent. Did she have a mousehole too? Seeing the danger that Molly posed to her, had she hidden somewhere safe?

Well, if she could do that, so could Molly—as soon as she figured out how.

The carving was followed by a handsome apparatus

made of gleaming brass that had something to do with ships at sea—but Molly still wasn't paying attention. She was deep inside her mind, hauling imaginary blocks of ice, piling one atop the other. Even if her wall was a failure and offered no protection, her thoughts (*Lift, stack; lift, stack; lift, stack*) would be as interesting as watching mold grow on cheese.

She kept it up for the rest of the tour, learning nothing whatsoever about the tapestry, the saltcellar, or the thumb harp shaped like a tortoise. Only when it was over and they were turning to go back did Molly realize that in building her imaginary wall of ice she'd forgotten about the kite.

"Wait!" Sigrid said. Everyone turned to stare. "I believe we've left something out. Mikel, weren't you telling young Marguerite about kites this afternoon?"

"I . . . yes."

"Well, apparently you piqued her curiosity. She mentioned it to me earlier—that she couldn't so much as imagine a kite and would very much like to see one. Isn't that so, my dear?"

Speechless, Molly nodded.

"It's just around the corner. What do you say? I'd hate for her to miss it."

This was so unlike the Sigrid they thought they knew, she of the closed expression and the acid tongue, that for a moment everyone was stupefied. But they quickly recovered themselves and agreed that certainly they could go see the kite.

Sigrid charged ahead and the others followed till they finally came to the famous kite from the land of Chin. As it had not been prepared for viewing, they set their small light-stones around it.

Molly didn't move. She just stared in disbelief. Why, it was just a toy, hardly bigger than a serving platter! True, it was shaped like a butterfly, and prettily painted; but beyond that it was nothing but sticks and paper. What a crushing disappointment!

"But—" She gasped. "That little thing couldn't carry a cat, much less a man!"

"It wasn't designed to carry a cat. Or a man."

Mikel cleared his throat. "I told her a story this afternoon, the one about the prince of Chin. . . ."

Sigrid nodded. "I know the one. An unusual choice, I'd think, under the circumstances."

"Yes," Mikel said. "A very poor choice indeed. But after I told her the story she asked me what a kite was, and I mentioned that we had one in our collection. She assumed it was the same one from the story."

"I can see how that would have happened," Sigrid said. "Well, Marguerite, that kite would have been much larger, with a sturdier frame, and made of stronger material. Silk, I'm guessing—something else that came to us from the land of Chin.

"Now notice that the kite has a tail. And while it's certainly charming, with all the little bows, it's not there for decoration. Its weight keeps the kite upright and balanced as it flies. Notice also that a string is attached, here at the front; that's how the flier controls the kite. By keeping the string taut, the flat surface is held against the wind, which then carries the kite up into the sky."

"Did the prince of Chin have a flier?"

"I expect his kite was of a different sort, more of a glider. You've watched birds soar?"

"Yes."

"Well, it would have been something like that."

"Ah," said Molly.

"That's it, then. Thank you all for indulging us."

They returned the way they had come. Light-stones in hand, they climbed the winding stairs, one at a time, back to the private quarters of the Magi.

You know, there's a science to building kites.

Sigrid was out of her mousehole again. Molly went on alert.

Why don't you try building some and see if they will fly?

Up, up, up they went, silent but for the tread of feet on stone. And Sigrid in her head.

There are books in the library on the principles of flight.

Molly turned and looked into that cold, expressionless face, now drained of the false cheer of only a moment before.

Yes, Molly said, without words. *I would like that very much.*

Sigrid just blinked.

❦ 28 ❧

A Visit from the Watch

RICHARD HAD BEEN OUT very late the night before, so he was hard asleep when the pounding started. He woke, confused. It was daylight, but a glance at the shadows outside told him it was early yet—too soon for the gentleman in the Old District to have noticed the rats, written out a summons, and had it delivered across the city to Neargate.

The pounding came again.

"Be right there!" he called, hurriedly pulling on his braies for decency. There was no time to dress; he'd have to go in his shirt. *Crikes!* Did they mean to break down his door?

He ran quick fingers through his hair, slapped himself on the side of the head to wake things up a little, then went to open the door. There stood a burly man dressed in the blue and gold livery of an officer of the Watch. His balled fist was raised, ready to pound again; and behind him stood two more officers.

"Good morning, gentlemen," Richard said, pointedly scratching a rib. "Rather early for a visit."

"We've come for the foreign gentleman." Before Richard could reply, they entered his house, stepping right around him. "Where is he?"

"Well, I don't know," Richard said, shutting the door and tugging at his shirt, which was embarrassingly short. "Lord Worthington took rather high offense at being lodged with the ratcatcher. So he cursed me to hell, then turned on his heels and went away. He hasn't been back since, and I can't say I'm sorry to see the last of him. Hope he went over the wall and drowned himself in the moat."

The watchmen exchanged suspicious looks. They didn't believe a word.

"Search the house," the chief officer said to one of his men. "You look around outside," he said to the other.

"What's the fellow done, officer? He's a lord, you know, not a petty thief."

"I know exactly what he is."

"A foreigner?"

"Right."

Richard stopped talking then and started thinking. Once you've committed to a lie, then you'd better arrange the furniture around it, so to speak. He did so now, because there were one or two questions he hoped he wouldn't be asked; but if they were, well, it would be better if he didn't have to come up with the answers on the fly. That's how mistakes were made.

"Mind if I finish getting dressed?" he asked. "I was still abed when—"

"Stay where you are. I have some questions to ask."

"Have a seat, then?"

"No."

The Harrowsgode Watch could be a stern lot, but never as hard as this. Tobias must be serious business, then.

"You were nosing around the university the other day, asking about the barrister."

"I'm allowed the freedom of the city so I can work at my trade. I have an official badge given me by the Council, attesting to my right—"

"Then you went over to the River District and were seen watching—"

Ah, one of the questions he'd been dreading, and

the furniture not yet in place.

"—a particular house belonging to—"

"Claus Magnusson, yes." Richard pressed his lips together and waited for the rest.

"And as it happens, a lady who was staying there is betrothed to this same Lord Worthington. All kind of suspicious, don't you think?"

"I do. Absolutely."

"Perhaps you'd like to offer an explanation?"

"Look, officer, I was instructed, very official-like, to give house-room to this Westrian gentleman. I got this letter—all loops and swirls and hard to read, not like the usual summonses I get, and delivered by a lad in livery riding a shiny new spinner. He was sent by a master barrister, name of Pieter. Well, I'm not used to none of that, see. And in the letter—besides the part where the barrister informed me I was to make the gentleman comfortable—he happened to mention that Lord Worthington was betrothed to the lady you just spoke of and said where she was staying."

Oh, please, please, don't ask to see that letter!

The watchman watched, frowning.

"So I was worried, as you can imagine—having lost the fellow on the very first day, and within an hour of his arrival—that I might be held accountable for it. It wasn't my fault. I was courteous as could be. And I didn't look like this, neither, when he came. I was dressed all properlike, not half naked, as I am now—"

"I don't want the story of your life, ratcatcher; just make your point."

"So I went there to find him." *Short enough?*

"Why?"

"To ask him to come back so I wouldn't be blamed on account of his leaving."

The watchman who'd been sent to search the house came back into the hall and shook his head. The chief officer nodded and returned his attention to Richard.

"We came here last night. Nobody was home. Where were you?"

"Catching rats. It's what I do, and night is when I do it."

"Where?"

Richard told him.

"Will this silk merchant vouch for you?"

"He will, and gladly, too. I caught thirty-seven rats for him."

"Where are they now?"

"The rats?"

"Yes."

"Buried in the rat-pit out back. I'll dig 'em up if you'd like to see."

"Did you go alone?"

Oh, crikes! Here was the other one! How he wished

he'd started with a better story! All the furniture in the world wouldn't make this one look good. But you can't put the milk back into the cow; he'd have to do his best with what he had.

"I brought my apprentice, as I always do. I'm required to have an apprentice by Harrowsgode law, so he can learn the trade and carry on—"

"What's his name and where does he live?"

Richard gave him the name and address, desperately hoping they wouldn't bother to contact the boy. Chances of that were good, especially after his client had sworn that Richard had been in his storeroom the night before, exactly as he'd claimed, catching thirty-seven rats.

The third man came in from the yard now; he hadn't found anything, either.

"All right," said the inquisitor, disgusted with Richard and bored with the whole business. "If you want to know, I think your story smells. I'd watch your back, ratcatcher, if I were you."

When the men had gone, Richard went into the pantry and sliced himself a large hunk of bread. He ate it quickly, leaning over the wash-sink. Then he got properly dressed and left the house.

❧ 29 ❧

Spirit Work

MIKEL WAS WAITING in the study-room, an open letter in his hand. He looked up when Molly came in, his expression grave.

"What?" she said.

"I have a message here. It seems you're to be moved from your quarters in the tower to a larger room downstairs—as you've apparently decided to take up kite building and will want to do some of the work in your chamber at night. Do you . . . is there something . . . can you explain this to me at all?"

"It's true. I do want to build a kite and see if it will fly."

"Instead of learning to read?"

"Can't I do both?"

"There are only so many hours in a day, and you're already so far behind—almost grown and just starting to learn your letters. To waste your precious time on children's games—"

"Who was the message from?"

"Sigrid."

"That's what I thought. It was her idea, you know."

"*Sigrid's* idea."

"Yes."

"Really?"

"Yes."

"Well." He looked away and sighed at the walls. "Who am I to question . . . ?"

"I only need a little help—just see if you can find some books about kites and the principles of flight, then read out the important parts. I'll do the rest on my own, in the evenings. In my new, large room. Then everything will be as before."

He nodded, tapping his knee with the letter—*slap, slap, slap*. He probed his teeth with his tongue and looked thoughtfully out the window.

"What? There's something else."

Mikel sighed. "The Great Seer has offered to begin your spirit work. He's too busy to take it on as a regular thing, but he wanted to get you started."

"When did this happen?"

"This morning. You've certainly captured every-one's attention."

"Mikel—"

"I know. And my answer is the same as it was last night. And there's something more, if you'll hear it."

She had the feeling she was going to hear it whether she liked it or not.

"Molly, you tend to say exactly what you think and show the world everything you feel. I'm sure you're just being honest and straightforward, and that's an admirable thing; but there's tremendous power in keeping your thoughts and emotions to yourself. Let others spill their secrets, then use what they reveal to your advantage. Think of it as buckling on your armor."

Molly was appalled. "I should be like that with *everybody*? I might as well be dead!"

"No, not with everybody. Just be careful whom you trust."

"I trust you."

"You do me honor, then. And, if you've been paying close attention—something else you need to learn—I have given you my trust as well."

"What about Soren. Should I trust him?"

He was quiet for a very long time.

"If you have to ask . . ."

⁓ ⋰ ⋱

Soren arrived a little after noon. There was a brisk, bustling air about him, as if he'd just come upstairs after a busy morning, which in truth he probably had. He smiled at Molly, not too broadly, friendly but not fawning. She decided that smile had been carefully chosen. Inwardly, she began strapping on her armor.

"Thank you, Mikel," Soren said with a curt little nod and a slightly altered smile—as between colleagues, though slightly dismissive. Mikel took the hint and left the room.

"Well, Marguerite, I'm quite looking forward to this. I hope you are, too."

"Yes," she said.

"So many new beginnings in such a short time."

She nodded, carefully arranging her expression.

"You are—as I'm sure you know—a very gifted young lady, with enormous potential. But a gift only grows into greatness through hard work." He raised his eyebrows as if to ask *Do you understand?*

"I'm willing to work. You won't find me wanting."

"That's what I hoped to hear. Now, let's suppose that I spoke to you in a whisper—*like this*. Let's also suppose that you were bustling about, gathering your papers together, sliding books across the desk, scooting in your chair—that sort of thing. Would you be able to hear me?"

"Probably not."

"Well, it's the same with the voice of your inner spirit. You must learn to listen for its faintest whispers—for unless you hear it calling, you can't draw it out and help it to grow. Do you see?"

"Yes."

"We're going to start with an exercise in stillness and concentration. I want you to close your eyes and let your muscles relax: your shoulders, arms, hands, neck, jaw, tongue, fingers, and toes. Imagine you're melting into the carpet."

He waited as she concentrated on one part of her body after another, bidding each to release and go limp. When Soren judged that she was fully relaxed, he began to speak in a soft, mellow voice.

"Now stay as you are, calm and peaceful; but I want you to move your consciousness away from your body. Empty your mind completely so it becomes like a great, cavernous space with a wide, welcoming door. Then you must have patience. Wait for whatever comes. And when it does, give it your full attention and hold on as long as you can. *Begin.*"

Molly was floating in a warm sea, deep below the surface. Everything around her was still. Soft light penetrated her world from above, but there was no sound except for her own steady breathing: in, out; in, out.

She drifted like this for a long time, as though in a dreamless sleep. Then gradually she sensed a change. She still floated, but now she felt the touch of fresh, cool air; and when she opened her eyes, everything was white.

She was in a cloud. It had dark places and bright places, soft edges and great patches of nothingness. And then it was gone. She squinted against the sudden light.

Her arms were outstretched, but they didn't feel like arms exactly. They were more . . . complicated. She turned her head and saw that they had become wings—glossy and black. They trembled with a subtle vibration, reacting to little movements in the air.

She angled her body and banked to the right—knowing how to do this without being taught—swooping down, circling the towers of Harrowsgode Hall, then rising again. She was conscious of every feather-twitch, each small adjustment she made in the set of her tail. It all came as naturally as breathing.

She looked down on the city spread out below her and the patchwork of fields in the valley. It would be so easy to fly there, to land amid the barley stubble. But why not go higher, farther, out over the very mountains themselves to the villages of Austlind and beyond, to Alaric in his garden back in Westria? How amazed he would be when she flew in!

But her wings weren't responding anymore; she couldn't move her primary feathers. They'd become nothing but outstretched arms again, she realized; and her hands were gripping something. Her chest and hips were cradled by strong bands. And above her, holding her aloft, was a great canopy of silk—the color of garnet, embroidered all over with sunbursts in thread-of-gold. New wings of her own design, the wings of a Magus Mästare. But they weren't as clever as her bird-wings had been. All they could do was soar, floating gently down, always down. . . .

Molly opened her eyes. A stack of books lay on the desk, and beside it a basket of materials for building a kite. Someone must have come into the room, probably knocking first, and put those things down on the table. Then whoever it was had gone out again and shut the door. Yet she'd heard none of it.

"How do you feel?" Soren asked.

"Fresh as springtime." She looked out the window and was startled. "It's almost dark!"

"Yes. You held on for a very long time."

"It didn't seem long."

"It never does."

She nodded. She'd spent a whole day flying.

"So, tell me," he said, leaning forward on the desk, wearing a friendly smile, "what did you see?"

Molly felt the hair rise up on her arms. Then, quick as lightning, the armor was back on again.

"I was in a barn," she said, "very big and very dark. And there were all these cows. . . ."

❦ 30 ❧

The Silversmith's Shop

RICHARD STOOD AT the entrance to a silversmith's shop, his hat in his hand. He'd been directed to go there by Molly, who'd sent another message by her raven.

He'd never been to this particular workshop before. He'd bought his own little treasures—the tray, the cups—in the Neargate District, where they didn't stare at foreigners or ignore them altogether as they did in the city establishments. So this visit made Richard uncomfortable. He'd had to nerve himself just to walk through the doorway.

"You the ratcatcher?" asked a very young apprentice,

noting Richard's cape and badge.

"Yes, I am."

"Well, you've got the wrong place, then. Nobody called you here."

"I'm not on official business," Richard said, feeling once again a boy of eight years, a lowly servant expected to bow and doff his cap to his betters.

"Then why have you come?"

"To spend my gold, lad—which I earned by honest labor in the service of Harrowsgode. I believe it's as good as any other man's."

The boy was taken aback by Richard's boldness. "Shall I call the master?" he asked.

"No. We won't bother him. I just want a few brief words with one of your fellows, Jakob Magnusson."

"Oh," said the boy. "He's over there."

"Jakob," Richard said, pulling up a stool and settling himself on it, "I have come at the request of a lady whose name I shall not mention." He kept his voice very low so only Jakob could hear. "She is related to you—a cousin, I believe."

"That lady is in no position to request anything, or send anyone anywhere."

"So one would naturally assume. All the same, she has found a way to get messages out of . . . the place where she is."

"Yet I still don't believe you."

"And why not?"

"Because she's just as incapable of writing a letter as she is of sending one."

"Well, see, that's changed. They've got teachers up there at . . . the place where she is, and she's rather a quick study. Now why don't we just move on to the point, which is this: the lady wishes me to ask you about a certain cup. How soon will it be ready?"

Jakob put his hand over his mouth, a small gesture of astonishment, then disguised it by rubbing his jaw. Richard had his attention now.

"I worked on it for a while after she left—or to be more precise, after my father arranged for her to be taken. After that there seemed no point. So I stopped." He gave a little snort and shook his head. "She wanted it for the king of Westria, you know."

"I was aware of that, actually."

"Well, the king won't be getting his cup, alas. My cousin isn't going anywhere."

Richard allowed a smile to creep onto his lips. He leaned forward and lowered his voice even further. "I wouldn't be so sure of that."

"What do you mean?"

"Exactly what you think."

"There's a plan?"

"Two."

Jakob started. "Two plans?"

"Think about it."

He did. It took a minute.

"One to get her out of . . . her current location, and one to get . . . away?"

Richard smiled and gave the slightest nod.

"Can you tell me what they are exactly?"

"No."

"Is time important?"

"You mean the cup? The answer is yes. The sooner, the better."

Jakob sighed, more in resolve than despair. "I still have the gilding to do on the base, and the last of the trim. Then there's all the enamel work—very precious business; it can't be rushed."

"How long?"

"A week, maybe more. I'll have to come in early and stay late. It's my own personal project and must be done on my own time." He smiled now. "Tell her I'll try to finish it in a week, and it will be *everything* she expects. Make sure you tell her that part."

"I will, and she'll be right glad to hear it. Now, there's one other thing. The lady has no access to her money at present—"

"I know," he said bitterly. "It's in her bag, with her

things, in my house."

"Yes, well, the point is that she has asked me to pay you myself, and she'll reimburse me later. I've brought—"

"Don't!" he snapped. "I owe her—*my whole family* owes her—far more than the price of a chalice, considering how she was betrayed. It disgusts me to live there. It'll be a pleasure to come to the workshop early and stay late."

"All right, then. I'll be back in a week to pick up the cup. In the meantime, if you should happen to be accosted by a raven—"

"Excuse me?"

"A raven, with a slip of paper wrapped around its leg—?"

"Of course!" he said, rather too loud. Then he dropped back to a whisper. "I understand now, about the messages. Very clever."

"She is, apparently—clever. Tobias keeps mentioning it."

"I'll be especially friendly to ravens from this moment on, though how this particular bird will know who I am and where I am to be found—"

"I'm sure it already does. This particular raven is also quite clever. If I didn't know better, I'd say it was a human living under an enchantment. Most certainly it serves the lady with impressive devotion. Now, I'd better go. You can frown when I leave, as though I forced my conversation upon you." Richard made to rise.

"Wait."

He sat down again.

"One last question. This plan . . ."

"Yes."

"Is it . . . limited? To the number of persons who can . . . you understand me?"

"I do. And no. It is not like . . . a boat, say, where there are only so many seats." He knew what Jakob was asking, but he'd let the boy do it himself.

"In that case, would you ask the lady if I might go with her?"

"I will, and I'm sure she'll say yes." Then, after weighing it in his mind for a moment, he added, "I'll be going, too."

❦ 31 ❧

The Tunnel

CONSTANCE ALWAYS SEEMED to know when morning had arrived, though the shed in which they slept was as dark as a cave, having no windows whatsoever. Perhaps she possessed some secret dog-knowledge to which he was not privy. Or maybe she just had better ears and could hear the cocks crowing in the village. However it was, Tobias could depend on her to wake him early by walking across his chest and nuzzling his cheek with her warm, wet nose.

He gave the dog a friendly squeeze and a scratch behind the ears, then sat up and felt in the darkness for the lantern and flint.

Richard was very particular when it came to his equipment, and he insisted that light-stones, while an admirable invention, weren't nearly bright enough for ratting at night. Nor could you adjust the degree of their light by turning a flame up or down as you could with a lantern. So he'd petitioned the Council for a special dispensation to continue using oil lamps, and his request had been granted.

When the room was lit, Tobias opened the rat-proof iron box and took out some bread and cheese. Richard always brought him the best his neighborhood cookshop had to offer: juicy meat pies, ripe cheeses, fresh fruit, plump sausages, and bread that was whiter than white—all a complete waste of money. It might have been cakes made of sawdust for all Tobias cared. Food was just fuel for his body, giving him strength for the labor ahead.

Having fed himself and the dog, Tobias dressed, rolled up his pallet, and stashed it in the corner along with the rat-proof box. Then he slipped on Richard's heavy leather gloves and went to work removing the boards that covered the entrance to the tunnel. Constance stood, her senses primed, her muscles quivering with desire. As soon as the first board was off, she shot through the opening like an arrow, scrabbling down the stairs and into the long, dark, wonderful hole where the rats lived.

When he had the entrance completely uncovered for the day, Tobias followed with the lantern, hunching over since the ceiling was low. His back ached constantly from working in that unnatural position. But Tobias didn't care about that, either. He just thought about the work.

When he and Richard had first started clearing the entrance, they'd noted with growing excitement that the walls and ceiling were sturdily constructed of stone blocks, most of them still intact. But breaking up the hard-packed dirt and rubble that filled the tunnel, then carrying it all out bag after bag, was slow, tedious work. And Tobias did most of it alone, since Richard had his two ratting jobs to attend to, plus disposing of the bags of rubble and running back and forth across town to get food and other supplies. If the tunnel was like this all the way through, the job could take a year or more—and even Richard couldn't explain *that* to the owner of the house.

Then one evening when Tobias was in the tunnel, working late, swinging his pick for the thousandth time that day, he felt the barrier give way. After that, he went at the little hole like one possessed until the opening was wide enough to reach his lantern through. Only then did he know for sure that they wouldn't have to dig the whole way out. As far as he could see by the lantern's light, the passageway was clear, if you didn't count the mess carried in by countless generations of rats, and their desiccated corpses, and the droppings they'd left behind.

"From now on," Richard had said when he'd arrived later that night, "we go at it quick and dirty. No need to clear out the muck. I seriously doubt your lady cares what she walks through so long as she comes out beyond the walls at the other end. We can finish the last bit tonight, you and me together—just enough to get through, that's all we really need. Then we go to work like demons on the far end."

Left hanging in the air, unspoken, had been the Great Uncertainty: what they would find on the other side. Tobias had tried not to think about it as he slammed his pick into the slowly receding back wall day after day. Yet think about it he had, asking himself how *he* would have gone about hiding the egress from a tunnel. He'd have rolled in enormous boulders to cover the fill, that's what; and the thought of that was horribly depressing: to work so hard and get so far only to run into solid rock.

Well, he told himself, they'd cross that bridge when they came to it. For now his mission was simple and clear: to break down the wall at the end of the tunnel, shovel the dirt and rocks into canvas bags, and haul them up to the storeroom for Richard to dispose of later. Then, after stretching out his back for just a moment, he'd go back in and do it all over again.

Constance helped break the tedium, trotting along beside him with her boundless energy, always on the lookout for anything ratlike, eager to show Tobias how beautifully she did the disgusting thing she'd been bred to do. (In addition to the bags of rubble upstairs, there was also a smaller one filled with the lifeless bodies of her vanquished prey.)

The "rat-muck" Richard had mentioned so lightly was more plentiful and revolting than Tobias could have imagined. The tunnel stank of it; so did Constance and Tobias. For all his care—leaving his boots and tools inside the tunnel at night, boarding it up, washing himself and the dog as well as he could with what water he had—the smell of rat urine was in his nostrils day and night.

And then there was that other thing, which was worse.

Richard had told him that the Harrowsgode folk thought plague was carried by vermin. Since then, the very sight, sound, and stink of rats became forever linked in his mind with a single terrible image: his parents laid out on their marriage bed, the baby placed between them, their spirits gone, their bodies ruined—and his little sister, Mary, not yet showing any symptoms, looking up at him and asking why Mama wouldn't get up and make her porridge.

But none of that erased the fact that unless they finished clearing the tunnel, they would never get out. Tobias would die, probably soon, and Molly would be a captive all her life. So he offered up his suffering as a sacrifice, knowing it to be superstitious nonsense, knowing that all the rat-stink in the world couldn't buy Molly's freedom. But it helped to play tricks with his mind, so he chose to think that way.

Around midday Richard arrived, more than usually jolly. He'd brought some pork pies for Tobias and a pig's knuckle for Constance.

"Sit down and have a rest," Richard said. "And have yourself something to eat. You'll be no use to anyone whatsoever if you pitch over dead from overwork. And you'll be in the way, too. We'll have to climb over your body on our way out."

Tobias laughed, feeling the tension drain out of him. He sat and ate as he'd been instructed—though not before washing his hands—and was quite miraculously restored.

Richard went on smiling. He plainly had something to tell and was waiting for Tobias to ask.

"All right," Tobias said, "what is it?"

"This!" He produced a strip of paper with an enormous grin.

"From Molly?" He took it from Richard's hand and saw that it was covered with words, not pretty written, but bold as brass—Molly through and through. He looked up at Richard pleadingly. *Don't tease me, not now! Just tell me what it says.*

This only served to encourage him.

"Now, you've told me rather a lot about that girl of yours, Tobias; and I confess I've doubted whether she could be as amazing as she's been presented: battling demons, rescuing princes—"

"Richard, for heaven's sake!"

"She's beautiful, of course, and clever, clever, clever—"

"I could strangle you with one hand, you know, while eating this pie with the other; and I'm quite inclined to do it, too, if—"

"Patience, lad. Who would bring you food if you strangled me?"

"No need. I'd slice you up and eat you raw."

"That's the spirit! I'll tell you—though, mind, this is something that deserves to be told right—"

"And you're the very man to do it."

"I am indeed. So here it is: your beloved has sent me to a silversmith's shop to see about a cup, which I have done. It will be ready within the week."

"That's why you're grinning?"

"No. I told you it must be enjoyed slowly, like a fine dinner."

Tobias glared at him in silence.

"What else? Let me see. She is gratified to know that you are safe and that we have found an escape route. I was so exceedingly careful in my choice of words, in case the message was intercepted, that I rather feared I might have been too subtle altogether. But she made my meaning out perfectly and was nearly as cagy in her reply, so that I had to read it over a time or two before I got it entirely straight in my mind."

Tobias folded his hands as if in prayer, the very model of quiet patience.

"Oh, dear, I shan't do it justice, but I really can't bear to drag it out."

Tobias raised his eyebrows, just a little.

"Prepare yourself, man, to be knocked over with amazement. Are you ready? You are? Good. Well *your lady*—who I have vastly underestimated, I confess it now, without reservation—is at this very moment . . ."

Tobias unlaced his fingers from their prayerful pose and reached out a hand as though to grasp something—a ball, say, or Richard's throat.

". . . is building herself some wings."

Tobias froze, stupefied. "Wings?"

"Yes, Tobias. Wings. *Your* lady is going to *fly* out of bloody Harrowsgode Hall. Now, what do you think of that?"

❧ 32 ❧

Wings

HER NEW ROOM WAS twice the size of her chamber in the tower. And while the windows there had been small and covered by a grille, here she had a large double casement. When both of the panes were opened, it provided a fine, wide sill—a perfect place to perch while arranging one's flying apparatus before flinging oneself off the building.

It was also a more comfortable spot for Uncle to land; he'd managed with difficulty before.

All she'd lacked was privacy, and that would be essential once she started constructing her Magus wings. To that end, she'd had a few words with the chambermaid, begging the girl to stay out of her room and never mind the mess. Because otherwise the maid was sure to tread on one of the kites, or be tripped up by a bit of string, or knock over a pot of glue. The girl had not minded in the least—that much less for her to do.

Now Molly sat on the floor with her pile of willow wands. Winifred had gathered them at her request; and Uncle had carried them by night, one at a time, to her new room at Harrowsgode Hall. Then he'd gone back to Winifred for one last package containing a penknife, a needle, and six spools of thread.

The choice of willow had been brilliant; it was supple, light, and strong. But tying the individual branches together to form a perfect curve, making sure that at each connection point the thread was wound tightly many times, then finished with a stout knot—that wasn't so easy. And her life would depend on having done it right.

She laid out the first willow branch on the floor, admiring its graceful curve. Then she nested a second one against the first and slid it down about a hands-breadth so that its thin end extended beyond that of the first. Now she bound them together at four points. In this way, with each addition, the structure would grow in length and sturdiness.

She worked in a dream state, with utter concentration, effortlessly harnessing something within her that guided her busy hands, correcting the shape of the curve as needed, alerting her if the thread was too loose at any of the connection points. When it was, she'd unwind it and start again.

Time was suspended. The slender moon, a bright shallow cup, hung motionless outside her window as she worked.

When the two wings were completed, their supporting struts attached and the trailing edges perfectly formed, they proved to be equal in length, exact mirror images of each other, each with a delicate curve from side to side and front to back, as when you cup your hands to splash water on your face.

Now she started on the central structure that would join the wings and support the harness.

Still the moon remained a fixed point in the sky. Still Molly worked under the guidance of her inner spirit. The world around her was hushed.

She'd reserved the thickest branches for this final step. Simple though it was—a box shape, longer than it was wide, reinforced by crosspieces and the overlapping origin of the wings—it had to be strong.

Her hands knew exactly what to do.

When at last it was finished, lacking only its silken

skin, she lifted it and felt its weight. It was heavier than she'd expected, but still she believed. From working with her kites she knew the astonishing power of wind against a broad surface. It would hold her weight and that of the wings, and carry them over the city walls to freedom.

As soon as the cup was ready, as soon as the tunnel was finished—then she would cut apart her beautiful Magus gown and attach the silk to the frame with careful stitches, using the scraps to form a harness—one loop to support her chest, one to support her hips, and a small handle on either side to grip with each of her hands.

Now she had only to wait, and sleep.

Outside, the little sliver of moon began to move in the sky again.

⚛ 33 ⚛

Rats

AS BEFORE, TOBIAS was alone in the tunnel when his pick bit through the fill.

He'd found the first stair earlier that morning and known that he was close. Perhaps by dusk, when Richard arrived, he'd have broken through altogether. Excited, he'd redoubled his efforts, clearing step after step.

But it was trickier digging up than it had been digging down. There was always the danger that a large chunk would break away from the wall and bury him in a heap of rubble. So the nearer he came to the top, the more careful and analytical did his process become—working in from the side, for example, instead of starting in the middle.

It was going well. He allowed himself to hope. Any minute now his pick might cut right through that wall like a knife through butter; light would come streaming in from the outside world, bringing with it the sweet smell of sun-warmed grass.

But instead his pick met stone, and the unexpected impact sent him tumbling down the stairs. He lay there for a moment, catching his breath. Then he got to his feet again and held the lantern up to the wall. There wasn't much to see. Stone, yes, undoubtedly—in one particular place. But that wasn't the whole story, not yet.

And the more he thought about it, the more hopeful he became. They couldn't possibly have moved a single boulder large enough to cover the entrance. It must be a pile of rocks, then, in varying sizes. There might be gaps between those rocks. Some of them might be small enough to move. To find out, he'd simply have to keep knocking rubble away till the true state of affairs was revealed.

He continued chipping away with the pick, exposing more and more rock. He worked all the way to the ceiling and found that the rock extended beyond the opening. He would have to work laterally, then. But nothing he found brought him joy. So far it was all the same: one single, enormous stone pressed against the opening.

Constance had been busy at the other end of the tunnel, doing what she did best. Now she came to join Tobias, bringing her usual offering.

"What a bloodthirsty, precious little monster you are," he said, using the point of his pick to fling the rat corpse off the stairs. Then he went back to clearing the stone, the endless, enormous, giant, hopeless—

Constance was at it again, this time over on the corner, right at the top of the stairs. She made a fierce little growl and began scratching frantically at the dirt with her forepaws. Well, Tobias thought, at least that was one section he wouldn't have to clear.

She barked twice, then returned to her digging: *scritch-scritch-scritch-scritch-scritch*—very fast.

Tobias stopped and stared.

Scritch-scritch-scritch-scritch-scritch! Bark-bark-bark!

"Constance!" he said, but she ignored him. Rats always came first. So he went and squatted beside her, loose bits of dirt flying out as she dug, covering his boots. Finally she reached the nest-hole and a rat darted out. Constance caught it on the run; and there followed the familiar screech, the creature's death throes, and then it was over. She dropped it, limp, on the flagstone. Another gift.

But this time the gift had been one of hope. Because a rat couldn't dig through stone any more than Tobias could. "My turn," he said, nudging the little terrier away with his foot so he could see what lay beyond the nest.

❦ 34 ❧

Messages

DEAR M.—

The vessel you ordered is finished, and the person who made it wishes to join us. Is this all right with you?

R.

Dear R—

Yes. Take him with you, and I will meet you at our destanashun. tamarro I think after noon mabe mid day.

M.

Dear Win—

I am redy. You need to by 2 more horses with sadels and have plenty of ~~proviz~~ food. Do this rite now. I will come tamarro after the mid day meal. Look up at the sky.

M

Dear M.—

Your gentleman friend wishes you to know that he is rather the worse for goose-grease, ashes, and rat-muck. He hopes you will not mind. He also says that if you die on him, he will never forgive you.

I cannot wait to meet you.

R.

Dear M.,

Everything will be ready. Be careful.

Yours,

Lord M.

❦ 35 ❧

Escape

MOLLY STOOD AT THE window watching the clouds. Uncle had said she must wait for the puffy kind, the ones that looked like mountains with flat bases, darker at the bottom. They were a sign that warm air was rising, and that meant perfect flying weather.

But she wasn't worried. She'd been watching for mountain-clouds every afternoon since Uncle had first mentioned them, and never had they failed to form. She recalled that it was Soren who managed the weather, and that made her laugh. If he only knew that he was making it easier for her to escape! Thunderclouds right now would be very inconvenient.

She'd been holed up in her chamber, the door locked, since dinner the previous night, at which she'd complained, in a loud voice, of a headache and a roiling gut. She'd spent the rest of the night taking her Magus gown apart and attaching it to the framework of the wings. It had been tedious work, stitch after painstaking stitch; but when she'd finished, Uncle had said it was perfect. She'd collapsed onto her bed, still in her clothes, and slept till midmorning.

Mikel, bless him, had knocked politely and asked if she was all right. But he'd woken her, and she'd been a bit snappish. *No*, she didn't want to eat. *No*, she wasn't up to studying today. *Please go away!*

She felt bad about that now. He'd been so kind to her. He'd taught her how to write her name and how to buckle on her armor. And now, if all went well, she'd never see him again. But she had the feeling he'd know that she was grateful even though she'd never said it.

The clouds were just about perfect now, the warm air ready to support her. She was ready, too. She'd plaited her hair and pinned it up so it wouldn't blow in her face. And she'd turned the skirt of her day gown into makeshift pantaloons by stitching it up the middle between her legs, fastening the hem tightly around the ankles and across the middle. It looked ridiculous, but at least her skirt wouldn't catch the wind and slow her down.

Now there was nothing left to do but lean on the windowsill, look at the clouds, and wait for Uncle. And that was hard. Molly was restless, and she couldn't stop thinking about all the things that might go wrong. It was a long list, and she had a gruesome imagination when it came to picturing disasters. What she really needed was to get this over with *now*, get up on that bloody ledge and bloody well jump off into—

There he was! Finally!

He landed gracefully on the sill beside her.

"Where in blazes have you been?" she scolded. "I've about lost my mind with waiting."

I was having a word with some rooks and jackdaws.

That left her more or less speechless. Saying goodbye to his little friends? Getting some tips on wind direction? "Well, I've been ready this last hour or more. Shall we go?"

Yes. But before you put the wings on, let's review this one more time: your window faces north, but you want to go south. So first—

"I know, Uncle: fly straight toward the mountains till I've caught the wind and feel I'm in control, then bank to the left, not dropping any more than I have to, and head straight south and over the walls—"

And the landing?

"It'll be hard, and I might tumble. I need to find a bare field, then drop down, arching my back at the last minute so the wings will tilt and slow my progress—then run."

Good. I believe you are ready.

It was harder than she'd expected. The wings were wider than the window opening, so she had to stand at an angle—one wing inside, one out. Just climbing onto the sill had been tricky since she'd needed to keep a grip on the handles so the contraption wouldn't slide down. Then once she'd made it up there, she had no way to steady herself; and the wind started tugging at the outside wing, throwing her off balance. She'd looked down, always a mistake, and was suddenly jolted by a moment of terror such as she had never known before—which, considering the life she'd led, was saying something.

"Uncle, am I going to die?"

No, Molly dear. You're going to fly. Just follow me.

He pushed off the sill and rose with beats of his powerful raven wings, then flew straight north. Now it was her turn. Molly took a deep breath, bent her knees, and sprang into empty air.

But it wasn't working, she realized with a stab of terror. She was falling, falling, falling—until suddenly there was a lurch and a loud *whomp* as the wind caught her silken wings, and fear gave way to elation. She was flying—the wind rushing at her face and lifting her up, the sun shining through the crimson silk like a blessing. *Oh, my stars,* she thought, *this is wonderful!* Up ahead, Uncle banked to the left and Molly followed, doing it neatly, staying high. She was in control. Like that ancient prince of Chin, she had harnessed the wind to do her bidding.

Below she saw rooftops, streets, people—and not too far ahead the city walls, and beyond them the fertile valley, greener than green. She began searching for a landing spot. Two or three stubble fields side by side would be ideal, in case she couldn't stop herself fast enough and had to keep on going. And it should be away from the village; she definitely didn't want to go crashing into somebody's chicken coop.

Suddenly Uncle gave a distress call—*Kraaaaaaw! Watch out!*—but Molly couldn't see any sign of danger. "What?" she shouted, her words almost swallowed by the wind.

Below, on the ramparts!

She saw the archers then, staring up at her, their bows drawn; and the first arrow had already been loosed. It missed, but the second one pierced her right wing, very near her elbow. And then, as if someone had written it there, three amazing words came into her mind: *Archers, stand down!*

To Molly's astonishment they *did* stand down, lowering their bows as one. But at the same moment she heard the sickening rip of fabric as the pressure of the wind tugged against the arrow hole, tearing the silk from the front edge to the back. She began to tilt, her balance lost as the right wing spilled air through the gap. She knew what happened to kites when they lost control: they went spiraling down with alarming speed till they crashed against something hard and broke into pieces. Now that was happening to her.

Except it wasn't. Something was holding her aloft, guiding her straight toward the valley. Above she could hear a fierce beating of wings—*whomp, whomp, whomp, whomp, whomp*! She looked up and saw bird-shadows against the garnet silk; and through the tear in the fabric she could see the movement of wings. Uncle's rooks and jackdaws, it had to be!

As she continued over the city walls, she saw the archers up close; they still gazed at her, but their threatening manner was gone. They simply gaped with amazement at the flying girl in Magus wings being carried by a flock of large black birds. Not something you saw every day, even in Harrowsgode.

Down they glided, quickly but gracefully, Uncle

still in the lead. He had chosen a landing spot and was guiding her there. Molly watched, her gut in a knot, as the ground rose up to meet her. *Arch your back,* she remembered, *then run as fast as you can.* But when? Now?

Never mind—they were doing it for her. The wings jerked back, rather suddenly, so that she was upright now, her legs circling in the air until the moment they touched the ground.

A stubble field is nothing like a smooth, flat meadow. It's all lumps and dips, and is full of hard, dry stalks. Molly staggered as she ran, twisting an ankle, the rough stubble catching at her pantaloons. She was going to fall—there was no help for it—and the whole apparatus would land on top of her, pressing her down into the dirt and the sharp things sticking out of it. But no, the birds still held her wings aloft, steadying her until she finally came to a stop, let go of the handles, and slipped out of the harness. They were like an army of very small servants helping a gentleman off with his cloak.

When she was free of her wings, they let the contraption fall and rose in unison. She looked up at them, raising her arms in gratitude. "Thank you, oh, thank you!" she called to the rooks and the jackdaws as they flew back toward the city, filling the air with their raucous cries. Then she trudged across the field in the direction of the village, Uncle still showing her the way.

Villagers had gathered outside their cottages to watch. They clapped and waved as she passed by. She felt for just a moment like a queen in procession—a very ragged queen with wild hair, dressed in pantaloons—so that she couldn't resist a few head nods, acknowledging their acclaim. When she saw Stephen running up the road to meet her, she laughed out loud.

"Stephen!" she shouted. "Did you see? I flew through the air!"

"Yes!" he said, breathless, taking her arm and urging her to pick up speed, hurrying her back toward the town. "It was astonishing—we really must hurry, my dear—and when the archers . . . oh, and the birds! Well now, *that* was something!"

"Are the horses ready?" She was gasping now, too.

"They have been since this morning."

"And everybody got out?"

"Yes."

"And Jakob has the cup?"

"Yes."

"Tobias? Is he all right?"

"Can you run, lady? We don't know what they're likely to do next now that they've seen you escape."

The others were already mounted, hidden behind a large barn at the very edge of town—Winifred, Mayhew, Jakob, and another man who had to be the wonderful Richard. Hanging on each side of his saddle was a wicker basket, each holding a little dog with pointed ears. Three riderless horses stood ready and waiting. That would be hers, Stephen's, and—

"Where's Tobias?"

"He stayed behind," the man who must be Richard said, "so he'd be there to help you if you didn't make it over the walls."

"And you let him do that?"

"I had no choice. He's bigger than I am, and very stubborn. But he'll be on his way now, I'm sure."

"Then we'll wait."

"No," Mayhew said. "We won't. We need to get up that blasted narrow trail and into the safety of the canyon before darkness sets in—or they'll lower their blasted drawbridge and send an army in our wake. Don't worry about Tobias. He knows the way."

"That makes perfect sense," Molly said. "Absolutely. You go ahead. I'll wait for Tobias."

"Oh, for heaven's sake, you're impossible!"

"Go!"

"I will not!"

"Suit yourself then. I'm not leaving without him."

Finally Mayhew took a deep breath, snorted, and directed his troops. "Stephen, you get the others up to safety. We'll follow as soon as we can."

Stephen nodded, and without a word he turned his horse into the road. The others stared at Molly, unsure what to do, until Mayhew roared at them to go and do it bloody quick.

"You take care, Molls!" Winifred said as they rode away.

"Don't I always?" she replied.

✦ 36 ✦

Skulking

TOBIAS HAD CALCULATED the probable trajectory of Molly's flight from the tower. From that he'd determined the most likely landing spot, in the event she couldn't make it over the walls. With this in mind, he'd chosen a good spot to hide: a cluttered yard behind a bakeshop in the southern part of the city. It had the advantage of being close to an alley, so he could run out quickly when the moment came. It also offered a good view of the towers of Harrowsgode Hall.

There he now waited, skulking in a dark corner, a cap pulled low over his head. He'd traveled there by night and had been waiting all morning, though she'd said she wouldn't leave till midafternoon. Several times people had come out of the bakeshop to use the privy, and Tobias would always duck behind a ruined butter churn. It was small and he was large, so half of him was still in plain sight, but so far no one had noticed him.

The shadows grew shorter, gradually moving from west to east, marking the passage of time; and still Tobias stayed at his post, gazing upward, going over and over in his mind the many problems that might occur. As each of them occurred to him, he searched for some way to help. But in this he was unsuccessful. If she'd been prevented from leaving, for example, or if she dropped like a stone to her death—well, there was really nothing anyone could do.

And then, finally, there she was, soaring out into the open from the back of Harrowsgode Hall with the savage grace of a hawk on the hunt, her wine-red wings, lit from behind, glowing like the sunset. Tobias reached the alley, then, sprinting out onto the road, followed her with his eyes. How splendid she was, so unbelievably brave!

But what was that—an arrow? Surely it was—yes! And there went another one, with a truer aim this time, barely missing Molly and tearing a wing. He started to run now, with such dangerous speed that people leaped out of his way as they would from a runaway horse. His heart almost burst with the effort. Then it registered on his consciousness that the archers had lowered their bows. But it was already too late; a wing was torn. . . .

What happened after that had been so miraculous that he and everyone else in Harrowsgode could do nothing but gaze in wonder at the flying girl with the wounded wing being held aloft by a flock of ink-black birds, floating over the great walls of Harrowsgode and out into the countryside!

Tobias turned and dashed back toward the tunnel. But he didn't get far before an officer of the Watch shouted and stepped in his way. Deftly, Tobias danced to the side and kept on going. Soon others joined the chase. He could hear their shouts and the sound of hurried footsteps. They didn't know what he had done that deserved pursuit, only that he was a foreigner, out where he didn't belong, and his behavior seemed suspicious.

Tobias ran with the endurance of youth, taking great strides with his long legs, drawing steadily ahead of the crowd. He was heading straight for the windowless shed where he and Constance had spent so many nights. He reached it, slammed the door behind him, and since it couldn't be locked from the inside, dragged a couple of rubble sacks over to block it.

But he doubted that would keep them out for long. There seemed to be a lot of them, and if they worked together they could easily push his makeshift barricade aside. Then they'd see the tunnel entrance straight ahead of them, and the chase would simply continue—down the tunnel, out the narrow opening, and into the village, complicating everyone's escape.

He found the lantern where he'd left it, just by the door, and lit it with the flint. Then he set it on the floor in the middle of the room, swinging down the metal shields on three of the sides so it would only shine straight ahead and not on the back wall where the tunnel entrance was. When his pursuers entered, they'd be blinded by the jarring blast of light out of a sea of darkness.

But that would only slow them down, he realized, and he needed to stop them altogether. He could hear their shouts in the distance. He probably had a minute, maybe a little more, before they'd have the door opened. He hauled another bag of rubble to his barricade. It might help a little. And as he was doing it, inspiration struck. He knew exactly what to do.

He grabbed another sack from the far corner and scattered its contents in a broad semicircle around the glowing lamp. He paused for the briefest moment to admire his ghoulish tableau: a sea of dead rats rather past the time when they ought to have been buried in the rat-pit—some of them bloated, all of them stinking, the whole lot of them brilliantly lit.

Thanking Constance one more time, Tobias fled, hands outstretched in the darkness, running—running through rat-muck, running toward the faint light that beckoned at the end of the tunnel.

❦ 37 ❧

The Canyon

MOLLY SAT SPRAWLED in the dirt, graceless as a guttersnipe—picking, picking, picking at the stitches that held her skirt together. If she was to sit in a saddle, they must come out. If she ruined her gown, so be it.

She was glad Mayhew was looking elsewhere—first at the castle gate to see if the drawbridge had been lowered, then to the western corner of the city walls around which he hoped to see Tobias coming, preferably very soon. Back and forth he went, from one side of the barn to the other, peering around the corner, saying nothing.

Rip, rip, rip, tear—Molly would break the thread,

then take hold of a free end and pull again, the fabric of her gown pleating itself until it would go no farther, at which point she'd break the thread and start again.

She heard a hiss from Mayhew. "I see him!"

"Tobias?"

"Yes."

He unhitched his horse and the other one for Tobias. Seconds later he was away, leading the riderless mount by the reins.

Molly gave her skirt one last heartless rip, then climbed onto her little mare and trotted after him, searching the landscape for any sign of Tobias. But she saw nothing. Mayhew must have the eyes of a hawk. And then she caught the movement, a head and shoulders plowing through a sea of barley. She set heels to her mare and caught up with Lord Mayhew as Tobias emerged into the lane. He stood there for a moment, gasping for breath.

"Merciful heavens, Tobias!" said Mayhew. "What have you been doing in there? You'll frighten the horses with your stink."

His hair—no other word would do—was disgusting: greasy, grimy, and matted. His clothes were soiled with sweat and filth, his face and hands covered with mud. And even from a distance they could smell the rat-muck.

"I've been digging a tunnel," Tobias said, looking not at Mayhew but at Molly, who was trying very hard not to laugh. Then, with all the dignity he could muster, he took the reins and mounted his horse.

❧ ❦

As they climbed the steep trail, Mayhew kept looking back at the drawbridge, and was astonished every time to see it still closed. Tobias was searching the west side of the city walls for any sign that his pursuers had made it past the rats to the tunnel, and noted with satisfaction that they had not.

But Molly just looked down at the beautiful valley below, and at Harrowsgode, the city of her people. As eager as she'd been to leave, being there had changed her; and now she felt a strange tug of sadness. She thought of all the people who'd been kind to her—Mikel, Pieter, Ulla, Laila, Sanna, Lorens—and knew she'd never see them again, would never know the end to their stories. Had William felt the same, she wondered, as he climbed this very trail on his way to a new life?

She saw her abandoned Magus wings, still lying in the stubble field like the carcass of a giant, dead insect. She hoped that someone would go out there and haul them in, use the beautiful embroidered silk for the bodice of a gown. That would be nice.

The sun had already dropped behind the western mountains, but it seemed rather darker than it ought to be. The coming of night, like the coming of morning, was gradual in the valley. Long after the sun set the sky would still be bright, slowly fading into twilight, then finally into the almost-dark of northern summer.

"I don't much like the look of that," Tobias said.

Looking up, Molly saw that the perfect mountain-clouds of less than an hour before had now turned heavy, lowering, and black. You never saw thunder-clouds in Harrowsgode, not at this time of year. So why now?

Her breath caught as she suddenly understood. She squinted at the distant towers of Harrowsgode Hall. She could almost *feel* Soren up there, watching their ascent, waiting for the perfect moment. Of course. He'd never had any intention of letting them leave. But how was she going to explain this to Mayhew?

The trail made another of its many zigzag turns. The enormous stone figures loomed straight ahead and they heard the first rumbling of thunder.

When they finally left the narrow trail for the wide, flat ledge above, Mayhew looked angrily around. "Fie on Stephen!" he said. "I told him to wait!"

"No," Molly corrected, "you said to take everyone up to safety. He probably wanted to get them through the canyon while there was still light."

"All right," he said, grumbling. "Let's go."

"No, wait. There's something I have to tell you first."

"Molly, it grows dark, and it's threatening rain."

"Yes. But this is important. And you're going to have to trust me though you won't—"

"Skip the preamble," he said. "Make it fast."

"I'll do my best. There's a man up there in one of those towers. He's a very powerful Magus, the Great Seer. He uses ancient magic to control the clouds." Mayhew stared at her, incredulous, just as she'd expected. Another growl came from the darkening skies. "Think—why didn't they send anyone after us? Because this is so much easier. All he has to do is wait till we're in the canyon, then send in a thunderstorm."

Mayhew was still staring, but he seemed to half believe her. At least he was turning it over in his mind. "Well, magical or not," he said, "I think we should stay here on the ledge until this storm has passed. We'll get wet, but we won't be drowned in the canyon."

"I don't know," Tobias said. "We're awfully exposed."

"What do you mean?"

"Lightning. Molly—can the Great Seer control that, too?"

Before she could answer, a thunderbolt struck, barely missing Tobias and throwing the horses into a panic.

"Let's go!" Mayhew shouted, and dashed into the canyon.

They rode as fast as they could, but the floor was covered with small, smooth stones that slid beneath the horses' hooves, causing them to scramble and slide.

"Can you swim?" Mayhew shouted back to Molly.

"No."

"Well, your horse can, if the rush of water doesn't overwhelm her. Stay on her back as long as you can. If you're washed away, then kick your legs and flap your arms. That'll keep your head above water."

"All right."

"Pass it on to Tobias."

She did.

Now it began to rain softly, the high walls of the canyon protecting them from all but a few errant drops. But they knew this was only the beginning. Soon it would start to pour, and the water would stream down the mountain slopes and into their narrow cleft in the rock—water with nowhere to go but out the two narrow passages, one on either end. It would rise with alarming speed, the space being so narrow, covering first the horses' hooves, then their knees, and then their chests. This would be no dip in a still-water pond on a warm summer afternoon; it would become a raging torrent, surging along the downward slope, carrying them with it to their deaths.

They urged their horses on as the rain picked up, little runnels already streaming down the sides of the canyon.

"Molly!" Tobias called. She turned to see him holding up his wineskin. Then he pulled out the cork and emptied it, and showed it to her again.

"What?"

He held up his hand: *Wait.* Now he blew air into it, his cheeks puffing out with the effort; the leather sack grew round as he filled it with his breath. Then, holding his thumb over the opening to keep it from deflating again, he quickly slid the stopper in and pressed it down hard.

"It'll float," he called. "Do the same with yours. Keep the strap around your wrist."

Molly nodded and felt for her own wineskin, but it was hard to concentrate now. The rain was coming down the cliff walls with tremendous force, beating on their heads, their backs, the tops of their knees;

running into their eyes and making it hard to see. She finally found the wineskin and did as Tobias had showed her. But half of the air escaped before she got in the stopper, so she had to do it a second time. Even then it wasn't as plump as Tobias's was, but she stoppered it successfully and felt its roundness. Better than nothing.

The horses pressed stoically on, heads down, heaving with the strain. Then a surge of water caught them from behind, lifting horses and riders alike, driving them forward, knocking them against the narrow walls as they went. Molly lost her wineskin and watched as it floated away. Her mare was paddling frantically, trying to stay afloat; but only her head remained above the flood. Molly could feel the force of the water tugging at her skirts.

"Stop it," she screamed into the darkness, "you putrid, stinking sack of maggots!" Water streamed onto her upturned face and into her mouth, making her gag. "You weeping sore, you pestilent toad. Do you *hear me*, Soren? You're nothing but an arrogant, stone-hearted, prideful old—"

Another surge came, and now she was out of the saddle, hanging on with only one hand. This part of the canyon was especially narrow; she was afraid of being crushed between her horse and the wall. And her gown, heavy with water, was dragging her down. She reached behind with her free hand and tugged at the sodden lacings, but they wouldn't budge. Then she was slammed against the wall again. *God's breath!* She would probably be crushed before she had a chance to drown!

If you are the great Magus I think you are, then you can find your powers even now.

She hadn't heard this exactly—the words had just come into her mind fully formed.

Such as *Archers, stand down!*

And *The girl has the brains of a goat.*

She gasped, trying to make sense of it while searching with her fingers for something, anything she could get a grip on.

But Molly dear, you will at least have to try!

"Well, yes, you *do* have a point there!" she muttered, finding a second handhold at last, a strap that had once held a basket of provisions. Then she drove everything else from her mind—the raging storm; the sound of Tobias screaming behind her; the heaving gasps of her poor, wild-eyed, overburdened mount; the absolute hopelessness of their situation—and dived deep into herself, deeper than she'd ever gone before.

She didn't feel the next great surge of water as it rushed over her head, slamming her against the wall;

she didn't see Tobias springing from his horse, beating the wild water with powerful arms, making his way toward her with desperate determination; she didn't feel his strong grip as he hauled her up onto the saddle, where she lay draped over it like a felled deer being carried home from the hunt. She was unaware of everything but the dark place inside her spirit and the thing that she had to do.

She pictured the looming clouds, heavy and black, emptying themselves of moisture in great, steaming, drowning gushes of water. Then she reversed it, and the clouds became a giant dishcloth, soaking up a spill from a giant kitchen table. She focused her mind on the rain as it began to rise in vast, beautiful, silver sheets, stroking them softly as it passed. She clung fiercely to her vision, eyes shut tight, teeth clenched, till the great black cloud had sucked up every drop that had fallen, then slowly faded and began to dissipate like morning fog.

Then all was silent. The sky was clear, ablaze with stars—and moving across that dazzling light show she saw the dark form of a solitary raven.

Well! That . . . was very . . . impressive!

◖ 38 ◗

Sigrid

SIGRID?

Of course.

You made the archers stand down.

Yes. But I take no credit for the birds.

You let me escape. You helped me escape. Why?

Because you wanted to. No one should be a prisoner, least of all you.

Soren tried to kill me!

I know. Because you destroyed all his plans and broke his heart. He thought he could mold you in his own image and use your powers against the forces of change. How ironic that you should be the one to bring him down.

But I didn't hurt him, not at all!

On the contrary, my dear; you destroyed him. Because you defeated him by feat of combat, he has lost his position as Great Seer. And because he used his sacred powers with the intention of taking lives, he will be banished from the Magi altogether.

I did all that?

All that and more; I think you may have saved Harrowsgode.

We've hidden behind our walls too long, living like misers, taking from the world and giving nothing back. It has weakened us, and what once made us great is dying. It's time we went out and engaged the world. It's time we opened our gates to let our restless spirits fly. Soren alone stood against it. Now everything is possible.

You aren't at all what you seem.

Neither are you, my dear.

I'm going to miss you, Sigrid; I never would have thought it.

Miss me—we've only just begun!

I don't understand.

Come now, Molly—do you really have the brains of a goat?

At the moment, yes. I probably do.

Through feat of combat you have taken Soren's place.

I'm on the Council?

You're the Great Seer of Harrowsgode.

Sigrid, no!

It's already done, my dear.

But why? Why would I want to rule a city that kept me a prisoner?

Because it's your ancestral home. Because there is so much here that is good, and we need your guidance. Because you were chosen to do it.

Well, I can't. I don't know how, and I won't even be there. I'm going back to Westria.

Your deputy can handle most of the work—meeting with the ministers, passing on the will of the Council, seeing to the general business of the city.

You?

Goodness, no. That wouldn't be appropriate at all. What I propose is that you choose a chief minister, someone who is not on the Council, nor even a Magus.

And you have someone in mind?

Yes. Prince Fredrik. By Harrowsgode law he is not permitted to rule while his father still lives; and since he's not a Magus he can't serve as Great Seer. But as your deputy, he can guide the city as he was born to do. It's quite legal, and it's what we should have done years ago—but Soren wouldn't allow it.

And don't worry. I'll guide you and teach you as best I can. I'll be by your side, watching you grow into your marvelous Gift. In return, wherever you might be, you will lead us out into the world.

But I think you've done quite enough for one day, and your young man seems to need some reassurance. I'll just slip back into my mousehole now.

Molly opened her eyes. Tobias was holding her close in his arms. It was hard to see his face in the darkness; but she could feel his grief. She could hear his sobbing breaths.

"Tobias, you're crushing me!" she said, her voice scarcely more than a whisper.

"Oh," he said. "Oh, Molly. I thought you were dead!" He touched her cheek and sobbed some more. "You didn't answer when I called."

"I was . . . busy, but I'm all right now. Just very tired."

"Look!" He gestured with his hand to indicate the dry stones beneath them, the bright, starry sky above. "That was you, wasn't it?"

"Don't tell anyone. You have to promise."

"All right."

She coughed and stirred, tried to get up, and found she didn't have the strength.

"Tobias, you're going to have to help me into the saddle. I don't think I can do it myself, and I want to get out of this bloody canyon."

He gathered her up as tenderly as a father carries a sleeping child, then gently set her down beside the mare. When she was steady, he laced his hands and leaned down. She set her boot into them, and he helped her rise till she could swing her leg over the saddle. He guided her feet into the stirrups and collected the reins, placing them in her hands. Then wordlessly he turned and walked back to his mount, knowing in his heart that she had passed out of his universe that night. She was beyond him now, and all the devotion in the world could never bring her back.

⚜ 39 ⚜

Incantations

SIGRID CAME AGAIN IN THE NIGHT.

If anyone had been watching, they'd have heard Molly talking softly in her sleep, would have noticed the restless movements of head and hands, the play of expressions across her face. But nobody was. They were all asleep.

She woke now and sat up, pulling her blanket around her shoulders and hugging her knees. For a long time she stayed like that, staring into the dying coals, trying to work out her story. When she was ready, she went quietly over to the clearing where they'd built their fire and ran her fingers through the dirt, searching for two smooth stones of equal size, smaller than a walnut but not as round.

Sigrid had been most specific, and Molly had feared she wouldn't be able to find them. Smooth stones were found in low places, where water ran. But they had camped on high ground. Yet there they were, side by side, half buried in the hard-packed earth at the very edge of the fire ring as though Sigrid had put them there.

She wiped them clean on her skirt. Then she held them as instructed—one in each hand, palms up— and began the Incantation of the Stones.

The words felt foreign on her tongue, and she didn't understand them. She'd merely learned them by rote, repeating after Sigrid many times. But when the stones grew warm and began to give off light, she knew she'd done it right.

She took a deep breath, shaking off her nervousness. This was a good beginning.

Now she went over to Tobias. Constance, who lay curled in the crook of his arm, woke and looked up; but he slept on, mouth slightly open, breathing heavily. The torrent in the canyon had washed him clean. His hair was tangled, but golden again.

With her right hand she carefully set the first stone on his forehead. With her left she laid the second on his chest, for remembrance and forgetting were matters of heart as well as mind. You cannot change the one without the other.

They glowed softly in the darkness.

Now she set a thumb on each stone and began the Incantation of Forgetfulness. It was longer than the first, and some of the words had to be spoken with an uplift of the voice while others slid down, then up again. She focused all her attention on doing it perfectly. Then she lifted her thumbs, lowered them again, and repeated the incantation a second time.

Tobias's heart and mind were open now.

"You will forget everything about Harrowsgode," she whispered, "even its name. You will forget that I flew from a tower and what happened in the canyon tonight."

Twice more she repeated the Incantation of Forgetfulness, and it was complete. She'd erased a part of his life, robbed him of memories. It was a heavy thing to do, and it frightened her. But she trusted Sigrid, and Sigrid had said it must be done.

Now came the final charm, the Incantation of Remembering.

Molly sang the magical words softly, in a pure, sweet voice. When she came to *aii-kah,* she remembered to press down on the stones, as one does when planting a seed. When she came to the word *chi-ahn-o,* she raised them to the skies, as if calling forth the sun and the rain.

Now she filled the empty spaces in his heart and mind with a new reality, a new memory. Tobias would go through his life believing it had really happened—and she could never tell him otherwise.

She'd never lied to Tobias before. She didn't like to do it now. But she did.

"We left Faers-Wigan and went to the town where my grandfather was born. It's to the north and east of Austlind, and it's called Einarstadt. We met my cousin Jakob there, and he agreed to make us a cup. But it took him several weeks, so we had to wait. Einarstadt didn't have an inn—it'd burned down the year before—so we lodged with the villagers. I stayed with my cousin. You stayed with Richard Strange. We all became very fond of one another, and they decided to come back with us to Westria. Now we're on our way home.

"That's what you will remember."

She gazed down at Tobias, deep in unguarded sleep, the little dog cradled in the crook of his arm and a small stone glowing on his forehead. He seemed at peace now, and she was glad, for those long days he'd spent in that tomb of a tunnel, alone but for Constance and the rats, digging his way out, fearing for Molly's safety, knowing he was powerless to help her, had damaged him somehow.

Now those memories were gone, and with them the pain. They were erased forever from his heart and mind. For good measure, just in case, she gave him one final gift.

"You were helpful to everyone, especially to Molly. You said funny things and made her laugh. And the whole time—every single minute, waking or sleeping—you were happy."

There. It was done.

As she sang the Song of Remembrance again, closing the loop and completing the enchantment, her voice broke; and she felt a wave of unaccountable grief pass over her. She didn't understand it, but it had something to do with the sweetness of his sleeping face and the surety that nothing would ever be the same again.

She removed the stones from his forehead and his chest. And then, impulsively, she leaned down and kissed his stubbly cheek. He sighed in his sleep and smiled.

❧ ❦

As the night drew on, Molly worked the same magic on Winifred, Stephen, and Richard, adjusting the story slightly for each one as needed.

Mayhew she'd left for last. And as with Tobias, she gave him an extra gift: a vivid memory of a day he'd gone out riding in the countryside. He'd been restless hanging around Einarstadt while Jakob made the cup, so he'd gone down to the river and rested there for a while.

Alaric had come into his mind then, and it had struck Mayhew suddenly, with the force of a blow, how very wrong he'd been about him. Yes, he was young and inexperienced in war, but he had a subtle mind and enormous courage. Mayhew might have acted as a father to the boy, supporting and encouraging him, helping him to grow into a great king. Instead, he'd schemed against him, mocking him behind his back and stirring up discontent among the nobles.

Oh, the tragedy of lost opportunity! He would confess it all to the king as soon as he returned to Dethemere. If it cost him his life, so be it.

Just then a fish had leaped out of the water, glittering silver in the afternoon sun—and Lord Mayhew had known, without the whisper of a doubt, that it had been a sign. Alaric would forgive him. They'd make a new beginning.

Molly smiled as she gave him this memory. It would do a powerful lot of good. It hadn't been part of the plan, and Sigrid might disapprove, but she didn't think so.

Now she sang the Song of Remembrance one final time. When she'd finished, Mayhew's enchantment complete, she left him and knelt in the grass, one stone in each hand, palms toward the sky. As she said the Incantation of the Stones in reverse, they grew dull and cold, their magic gone. She put them back where she'd found them and went to sit beside her cousin.

～❧～

"Jakob," she whispered into his ear. "Jakob!"

"What's the matter?" he said, startled.

"Shhh. Don't wake the others. I have something to tell you."

He rubbed his face, then sat up and crossed his legs.

"The secret of Harrowsgode is safe now," she said. "I laid an enchantment on each of them, removing all memory of their time in the city. They think we've been in a place called Einarstadt, in the northeast corner of the kingdom. Try to remember the name. That's where we met you and Richard."

"They taught you that at Harrowsgode Hall—how to do spells and charms?"

"No. I learned it from Sigrid tonight."

"Sigrid Morgansson? Of the Council?"

"Yes."

"Is she hiding behind a bush somewhere?" He smiled as he asked it.

"No. She's here. And here." She touched her head and her heart, knowing that he would understand. "She guides me now."

"You are a true Magus Mästare, then, whether

you're in Harrowsgode or not."

"I'm more than that, as you shall hear. But listen, Jakob. Wouldn't you like to see Laila again? See Sanna all grown up? Lorens, too—maybe in garnet robes next time? You might even find it in your heart to forgive your parents. I have."

"Don't, Molly! Do you think it was easy for me to walk away from them like that, knowing I could never return?"

"But you can—that's what I'm trying to tell you. Something happened tonight that changes everything. Jakob, remember in the garden when you said Harrowsgode folk only clasped hands with those they love and trust?"

He nodded.

"You said it was because Harrowsgode folk reveal ourselves when we touch; and for those with the Gift it comes pouring out of us like —"

"—water running downhill."

"—laying all our secrets bare. Well, tonight I'm like that water, so full of things to tell you that it wells up in me fit to bursting and must come rushing out. I ask you to clasp hands with me tonight, as cousins, with love and trust. And I will show you everything."

Then she reached out her hands, and Jakob took them.

❦ 40 ❧

The Cup

THEY'D ARRIVED AT THE INN late that afternoon. Dinner was over now, the landlord had cleared away the dishes, and the others had gone upstairs to bed. Only the cousins had remained behind.

Jakob held a plain wooden box. It had been beside him on the bench all during dinner. Now he handed it nervously to Molly, wishing there'd been time to commission a proper presentation case—something made of ebony, say, carved with initials or a coat of arms.

She looked up at him and smiled.

"Go ahead," he said. "Open it."

She took off the lid, handed it to Jakob, then lifted

out the package that lay nestled inside.

He'd wrapped it in layer after layer of silk, each of a different color, so that first there was emerald green, then scarlet, then saffron, then robin's-egg blue. Molly admired each one—so lovely—but really, he needn't have gone to all that trouble!

The final layer of silk—cloud white—dropped into her lap, and at last she held it in her hands: the Loving Cup. And it was a marvel.

The base, bold and masculine, was gilded and embellished with translucent enamels, pictures of delicate flowers and mythical beasts, framed in silver filigree. But the bowl of the cup was disarmingly simple, made of beaten silver. So perfect was its shape and size, so glorious its luster, that the base with all its knobs, and cartouches, and ornate decorations seemed to be reaching up in praise of the vessel itself, which was too perfect to require any ornament at all.

Molly said not a word, just laid the cup in her lap and gazed thoughtfully at the fire. Jakob felt the waves of disappointment rolling off of her.

"It's not right, is it? There's something wrong."

Still she was silent.

"I tempered the metal with my blood, just as William did."

"It's beautiful, Jakob," she finally said. "A masterpiece. A fitting gift for the greatest princess in the world."

"But . . ."

"That's all it is. A sip from this cup will not join two people together for life."

"Are you sure?"

She nodded. "Jakob—is this the cup you saw in your vision?"

"Yes. To the last detail."

"The inside of the bowl was silver, not gold?"

"Absolutely. That isn't what you saw?"

"No. In my vision, it was gilded. It glowed like the very sun."

"I don't understand that."

"Nor do I, but it has to mean something. You were supposed to make this cup, just as you saw it. And I was meant to give Alaric . . . a different cup. . . ."

"No," he said, "the same cup. It just—"

"—isn't finished!"

"Yes. I was meant to do what only a silversmith can. And I did. I made the cup that was shown to me in my vision. But *you* saw the cup in its final form. Molly, we were meant to finish it together."

"But how?"

"You'll see," he said.

⊰ 41 ⊱

Blood and Fire

THEY SAT SIDE BY SIDE at a long worktable, each wearing a leather apron. They were in a famous goldsmith's workshop that had served the royal house of Westria for many generations. But on this particular day the shop was quiet, the apprentices and journeymen off for the day and the doors shut to customers. Molly and Jakob were alone there except for the master goldsmith, who sat politely at the far end of the table and never left off watching them. They'd paid him handsomely for the use of his shop; but he didn't know them, and he had a fortune in jewels and precious metals to protect.

"In this bowl," Jakob was explaining to Molly, "we have powdered gold. And in this one we have mercury."

"It looks like liquid silver."

"Yes. It's called 'quicksilver' for that very reason. Now in a moment I'll heat them both in the furnace. The gold will melt into a liquid, and the mercury will become thinner and more watery. Then I'll mix them together—six parts of mercury to one part of gold."

"What am I supposed to do? We were meant to do this together."

"And so we will," he said, pulling his knife from its scabbard and setting it down before her. "We'll start right now, in fact—because there's a third ingredient that's not in the usual formula."

She cocked her head.

"Blood, Molly—remember? And apparently it has to be yours. That's why you saw gold inside the cup when I saw silver. The enchantment comes with the gilding."

She nodded, then studied her hand, back and front. At last she took up the dagger and made a neat slice, not too deep, right over a web of tiny veins near the spot where her thumb met the wrist. Holding her hand over the bowl, she watched the scarlet drops fall onto powdered gold. When she judged it was enough, she looked up at Jakob, who was ready with a strip of gauze to bind her wound.

"Excuse me," said the goldsmith, rising to his feet. "Why did you do that?"

"Ah," said Jakob. "We temper the metal with blood. An old trick from Austlind."

"Wouldn't chicken blood do just as well?"

"No doubt. I didn't think you'd have any on hand."

"But the lady—"

"The lady is fine," Molly said.

He sat down again.

Jakob set the two bowls into the forge with tongs, then pumped air onto the coals with a bellows. When enough time had passed, he removed them again and set them on the table. Then he poured the molten gold into the bowl of mercury, raising up a cloud of smoke.

"Now stir it with this," he said, handing her an iron rod. "Faster. Mix it really well."

While she stirred, Jakob opened the box that held the cup. He made rather a ceremony of removing the silk wrappings, for the entertainment of the goldsmith, who was leaning forward now, curious.

"Where did you get that, young man?" he asked.

"I made it," Jakob said, smiling at the man's astonishment. "Now, I'll need some aqua fortis, if you please, to prepare the cup for the gold. And a strip of chamois too."

When the inside of the cup was ready, cleaned of oils and dirt, the surface bitten by the acid in the aqua fortis so the gilding would stick, Jakob squeezed the mercury out through the chamois, leaving mostly gold behind. It was thicker now, the consistency of butter, and yellower than before; but it didn't really look like gold.

"Don't worry," he told Molly. "There's still a lot of mercury in with the gold. We'll burn it off in a minute. But for now we have a nice soft paste you can easily paint onto the cup."

"Me?"

"Yes. I'll show you."

Molly worked with careful, patient strokes, smoothing out ridges, filling in any spots she'd missed. But it wasn't perfect, and it didn't look gold.

"Well done," Jakob said, making a few minor touch-ups.

Once again the goldsmith interrupted. "Excuse me, young man, but I'm a bit concerned about your enamels. Might I suggest—?"

"It's all right. I have a solution. See what you think."

"What's the matter with your enamels?" Molly asked.

"We have to heat the cup to drive off the mercury. It'll turn to smoke and fly off into the air, leaving just the gold behind. Normally we'd put the cup right into the furnace, but we can't do that because I've already done the enamels; and since they're made of glass, they'll melt. But we can work around it. It'll take a lot longer, and we'll sweat like a pair of lost souls in hell; but it's more poetic, I think. You shall hold the fire, and I shall hold the cup."

Jakob took a clean linen cloth and folded it, as though to make a bandage or a blindfold, and tied it around Molly's mouth and nose to protect her from the fumes. Then he made a mask for himself. Finally he wrapped the base of the cup in many layers of wet rags to keep it cool and to protect the enamels.

"All right, cousin," he said, "I want you to take those tongs and find yourself a nice, hot coal. Good. Now hold it inside the cup, but try not to touch the surface of the gold. It's not easy, I know. I'll take a turn when you get tired."

It *wasn't* easy, and it took hours. Their arms ached, the fumes stung their eyes, and the heat was almost unbearable. At one point the goldsmith offered to help, but Molly sent him away. And slowly, coal by coal, the mercury was driven off into the air, leaving gleaming gold behind.

"What do you think?" Jakob said as he wiped the cup clean. "How does it look?"

"It glows like the sun."

"Pick it up."

"I don't need to. I already know the answer."

"Pick it up anyway. I want to do this properly."

"All right." She stood and held the cup exactly as she'd seen him holding it in her visions, at about chest height, like an offering. "This chalice," she said softly so only he could hear, "is not merely a beautiful work by a great artist; it is a true Loving Cup. It has the power to bind two souls together for life, to bless their children and their children's children down through the generations. Thank you, Jakob."

While Molly was wrapping the cup in its silken swaddling clothes, the goldsmith came over to Jakob. "Are you a licensed journeyman, lad? I believe you must be, though you look quite young."

"I've served out my apprenticeship, but I left Austlind before I was able to prove my competence."

"Would you like to work for me? I'll see you through the approval process with the guild. It should be easy. You have only to show them that cup, and they'll grant you journeyman status right away."

"The cup is not available," Molly said. "It's a gift for the king."

"For the king! Well, I imagine he'll be very glad to own such a beautiful piece."

"He will," she said. "I'm sure of it."

"Then you'll just have to make something new. I'll pay you full journeyman's wages, right from the beginning, even before you receive your papers. Watching you just now, I was most impressed."

"He isn't interested," Molly said, setting the lid on the box.

"I don't mean to offend, lady, but shouldn't the young gentleman speak for himself?"

"I suppose. But I rather think he'll be setting up his own shop. He'll be coming into a lot of money soon. The king is famous for his gratitude."

"A partnership, perhaps. We might consider—"

"Thank you, Master Goldsmith, for your generous offer. And thank you, Cousin, as well. But I'd rather wait a while before deciding what to do. I just might be going home."

❦ 42 ❧

Once Again in the Garden

THE GARDEN WAS FADING now. The roses and the lilies were over, and some of the beds were bare, the withered plants cut back to the ground. But the trees were bursting into autumn color. Red and yellow leaves covered the ground. As they walked the paths arm in arm again, Molly could feel the change. The world was shifting toward winter.

Nothing in nature ever stayed the same. Not even Alaric. Not even Molly.

"Stephen says you returned three days ago," said the king. "I'm sorry I wasn't here. I was up north hunting, if you can believe it, entertaining a pompous duke and a brace of arrogant lords."

"Did you kill anything?"

"I did, much to the astonishment of my guests, who think me a pup and a weakling—though one could hardly grow up at King Reynard's court, as I did, without learning how to use a bow."

"It was a success, then?"

"No one pulled a dagger on me."

"Is it really that bad?"

"No. I exaggerate. A little."

He ran his fingers through his hair, thinking.

"Molly, I had a private interview with Lord Mayhew this morning. At his request."

"I see."

"Yes, I imagine you do—better than I, most likely. I should have been more forthright with you, about why I chose him to guide you into Austlind."

"That's all right. I figured it out."

"You did?"

"It wasn't that hard. How did the interview go?"

"I won't reveal everything he said, though I doubt any of it would surprise you. He confessed things to me that he needn't have, practically laid his head out on the chopping block and invited me to have the thing off. Pride, I suppose. He's a man of honor, determined to take his licks when he feels they're deserved."

"And?"

"I forgave him, and he was grateful. He knelt, and kissed my hand, and swore his undying fealty. I rather think you had something to do with all that."

"In a roundabout sort of way."

"Then, once again I am in your debt. I don't know how I would have managed if he'd gone on working against me like that, stirring up ill feeling. I might have had an insurrection on my hands—on top of my cousin Reynard nipping at my heels. Now I have a very useful ally where I once had an enemy. All thanks to you, Molly. I sometimes wonder if there's anything you cannot do."

"A bargain, Your Highness?"

"A bargain?"

"I'll stop blaming my upbringing, such as it was, for my every rude remark if you'll stop saying that I can work miracles."

"But I truly believe you can."

"And I truly believe that I was ill raised."

"A bargain, then." Alaric smiled as he said this, but the smile slipped quickly away.

He'd grown solemn since becoming king, but he was more solemn now than before. The weight of responsibility, which had come to him so tragically and while he was yet so young, was with him every hour of the day. It had snuffed out the bright joy that once had been a part of his nature. For never was there a more ardent king, determined to rule with wisdom and courage, no matter what it cost him. He looked older now, and exhausted.

"Stephen's not really your valet, is he?" she said.

He stopped on the pathway, threw back his head, and laughed. "No, Molly, he is not. When my parents sent me to Austlind as a boy, they sent Stephen, too—as my 'minder,' to make sure I didn't disgrace myself at Reynard's court. In time he became more like a father. Now he is my close adviser and trusted friend. Acting as my valet gives him good cover. People discount him and speak freely when he's around—just a servant, you know. It's very convenient."

"I can see that. I like him very much."

"I thought you would. So—that box you're carrying. I assume it holds the cup?"

"Yes. Why don't we go over to that bench by the pond. It'll be easier for you to open it if you're sitting down."

"All right. But tell me, is it the real thing? Made by your grandfather?"

"Yes and no. It's the real thing, but my cousin Jakob made it. And don't look so disappointed. It was made especially for you."

They turned a corner and walked through the boxwood arch. Straight ahead was the pond, the stone fish still standing on its tail, still spouting water. They sat on the bench, and Molly handed Alaric the box.

"Jakob wishes me to tell you that he's sorry the case is so plain. There wasn't time to order a proper one."

"It doesn't matter. I'll have a cabinetmaker build me a presentation case, with the arms of Cortova on it and Elizabetta's initials."

He took off the lid and started unwrapping the layers of silk.

"It's very powerful, Alaric. The bond it forms can never be broken."

He looked up at her. "What are you saying?"

"Just use it carefully, that's all. Use it wisely."

"That has always been my intention."

"Good. Because once the princess sets her lips to the cup, there's no turning back."

"I will take that under advisement."

The last layer of silk came off, and now the cup was revealed. He held it up to the sunlight, turning it in his hands. "Your cousin made this?"

"Yes. And he refused any payment. I believe a handsome reward might be appropriate."

"Without question. This is astonishing work. I am overcome."

"And while you're at it—being generous, I mean—you might do something for Richard."

"The ratcatcher who followed you home? Why?"

"Because you're in my debt, and that's how I wish to be paid."

"Are you *serious*?"

"Yes."

"All right, then. What does the fellow want?"

"Nothing at all. This is entirely my idea, and he doesn't know I'm asking. Alaric, Richard is an amazing man, very generous and kind. A good storyteller, too. He entertained us wonderfully on the road during our return. But he told me one story in private that wasn't comical at all—quite sad, in fact—about his childhood. And, well, it set me to thinking."

"What?"

"I believe Richard would find it . . . very amusing, and deeply satisfying, if you were to make him a lord."

The king laughed at that quite merrily. "Sir Richard, Lord Rattington?"

"Perhaps something a little more conventional would be better. Alaric, I *did* think twice before asking this of you. I know you're in a delicate position just now, and you took a risk when you raised Tobias and me to high estate. But perhaps you could do it quietly, not call undue attention to it. And you needn't give him lands or a house. He'll be staying on with Tobias at his estate."

"All right, then. Consider it done."

She grinned. "You will make a good man very happy."

"Then I'm glad it's in my power to do so. Now listen, Molly. I'd like you to remain at court this time and not go back to Barcliffe Manor. I trust you will not mind."

"Not in the least."

"The others may go home, of course—Winifred and Tobias. And I have *nothing* against the boy, Molly. I just don't need him."

"I understand you, Alaric."

He studied her for a moment, his head cocked at an angle. "What have they done with Molly, and who is this person they've put in her place?"

She laughed.

"Truly. You've grown up in—what has it been? Five, six weeks?"

"Horse flop! I'm just not my usual annoying self today. And I brought you the thing you wanted."

"Oh, Molly—*please* don't play a part with me."

"I'm sorry. I did it out of habit. It's . . . my armor."

He was looking at her now straight on, with something on his face she'd never seen before. It was the most intimate moment they'd ever shared. Molly felt as if she'd taken in a deep breath and couldn't let it out.

"Something happened to you in Austlind," he said.

She didn't speak. Still he held her eyes.

"And it's changed you. It lifts you up, even as it weighs you down. And you can't tell me what it is."

Oh, help me, Sigrid! Molly thought.

"It has set you on a path for life and laid a great burden on your shoulders. It was thrust upon you unexpectedly, but you accepted it all the same."

Sigrid? Is it permitted?

"It came at a heavy price. And now it's breaking your heart."

Do you trust him to keep our secret?

Oh, yes! With all my heart!

Then what are you waiting for, child?

❦ 43 ❦

Ravens

HE'D ALREADY SAID his good-byes, but he had to see Molly one last time. So he circled Dethemere for several hours till he saw them in the garden. They were sitting together on the bench beside the pond. Neither of them looked up.

So he rose into the sky and banked toward the east. He knew where to find her, and it wasn't far. She'd promised she would wait.

Soon they would soar through the skies together again side by side, dancing in the air, dropping and rising, one form mirroring the other. They would lock their talons and fly in loops, like a pair of acrobats. It would be wonderful.

Then they'd find a home and build a nest. She would be his, and he would be hers, for as long as they lived. A bond that could never be broken.

And at last he would be complete.

Don't miss the thrilling conclusion to Molly's story in

The

Princess
of Cortova

Premonitions

THE KING OF WESTRIA knocked on the door to Molly's cabin and was admitted by her attendant.

"Your Grace!" said the lady, blushing and dropping into a very deep curtsy.

"Leave us" was all he said, and she did.

The king crossed the room—it only took two steps—and stood over the little cot, examining the disheveled heap of bedclothes. He touched the blanket and encountered a shoulder.

"Molly?" he said.

She grunted softly.

"You are aware, I believe, that protocol requires you to rise in the presence of your king." When she answered this with a derisive snort, he grinned. "You could at least sit up so I can see your face."

"Not worth looking at," she mumbled. "And besides, I'm not sure I can."

"Then I shall help you."

He threw back the blanket and took her in his arms, lifting and settling her in a seated position as easily as if she'd been a child. He tucked a pillow behind her back, then drew up the covers again.

"You *are* a mess," he agreed, brushing tangles of damp hair from her face.

"Just the dried husk of my former self," she said drowsily, "hollow and crumbling to dust. Soon the wind will come and blow me away."

The ship lurched. She shut her eyes and furrowed her brow. "How is it that even though I'm emptied out entire, I still feel like I'm going to puke?"

"It'll be over soon. We're due to reach port tomorrow."

She swallowed the bile that had risen in her throat and shuddered.

"Have you been drinking the restorative I sent? You must have fluids, Molly, whether you eat or not."

"I had some of it this morning. Tobias all but forced it down my throat."

"Good for Tobias. I shall do the same. Where is it?"

She responded with a feeble wave in the general direction of her knees.

"What, under the *bedclothes*?"

"It's in there somewhere, I think."

"Oh, for heaven's sake!"

He pulled back the covers again and searched—muttering to himself about the indignity of it all, and how in blazes had it come to this?—till at last he found the bottle wedged between the bulkhead and the mattress.

He rescued it and removed the cork. Then, taking Molly's chin in one hand and the bottle in the other, he tipped a little liquid onto her tongue.

"Just sip it; that's right. If you take it a bit at a time, you're more likely to keep it down. And just so you know, you're going to finish this bottle before I leave. Then I will send you another. You'll drink that one, too. Understand?"

"Alaric, I really need—"

"I know. Tobias told me." He dragged a chair from the corner and sat down beside the cot. "One more sip, and I'll hear you out."

She drank it, fought off another a wave of nausea, then took a deep breath and looked squarely at the king.

"Alaric," she said, so softly that he had to lean

forward to hear, "you know how, before a storm, the clouds build and grow dark, and the wind picks up and feels suddenly cooler—it even has a different smell? You can feel in your bones that it's going to rain, and rain hard. Well, sometimes it's like that for me. I get a powerful foreboding of things to come. It looms over me like a storm cloud. That's how it's been these last days, ever since we set sail."

He nodded, all attention.

"Last night I had a vision—I've learned to tell the difference now between commonplace dreams and visions that come to me in my sleep."

"And this was a vision."

"Yes, a very strange one. I was in a garden—like in the abbey, remember? With covered walkways on all four sides? Only this was small. There was a pool in the middle, and there were lots of flowers. I was alone except for a very big yellow cat, and he was speaking to me."

"The cat?"

"Yes. He said, 'In chess, the object of the game is to protect your king.'"

"Molly, that's nonsense."

"Wait. I'm not finished. I said, 'I'm not playing chess—I don't even know how—so why are you telling me that?' And the cat started pacing back and forth, but he didn't answer. So I asked the question differently, because I thought I already knew the answer. I said, 'Are you warning me that my king is in danger?' And he said, 'Yes.' Then I asked him what kind of danger, and he admitted he didn't know, not yet at least. It could be that the danger was still forming. But he'd hoped I might be able to figure it out. And if not, well, at least I could warn you to stay on your guard."

"That's it?"

"No. There's more. I felt—in this vision—as if I were about to leave, but the cat was calling me back. He said, 'Didn't you wonder why King Gonzalo insisted that your king come in person to discuss the terms of the marriage and the alliance? Is that the way such matters are usually arranged?' And I said that as far as I knew—which wasn't very far at all—it was more common to work things out through messengers. But as it happened, going to Cortova was convenient for my king. By which, of course, I meant that you have to give the Loving Cup to the princess in person in order for the enchantment to work. But I didn't tell the cat that part, because I wasn't sure I could trust him."

"Molly, I'm trying very hard to take this seriously, but do you have any idea how comical it sounds?"

"Of course I do. But I'll let you judge when I've told you everything."

"All right."

"So the cat said, 'Think, Molly. Gonzalo neither knows nor cares that it's convenient for your king. In fact, he believes just the opposite, that it's a long journey at an awkward and dangerous time for him to be away, considering how things are between Westria and Austlind. So oughtn't you ask yourself why?'"

She'd been speaking with her eyes closed; it helped her concentrate. But now she opened them and looked directly at Alaric. She could see that he was considering what she'd just said, and that it had alarmed him.

"So the cat asked, 'Are you aware that King Reynard of Austlind *also* seeks an alliance with Cortova and hopes to marry his eldest son to the princess?' 'Yes,' I said. 'We've heard that rumor. But if they'd already come to terms, Gonzalo wouldn't have summoned Alaric, so that obviously means—' But the cat didn't even let me finish. He said, *'Really?'* and gave me this knowing look. 'Are you *sure?*' And that's when I started to put it all together."

"Molly, are you—was the cat—suggesting that Cortova and Austlind have already formed an alliance; and as part of their arrangement, Gonzalo has lured me away from home so Reynard can attack my kingdom?"

"That was my first thought, yes. But then—"

"What?"

"I reminded myself that Lord Mayhew remains in Westria, and you'd defer to him in military matters anyway since your skills don't lie in that direction. So your absence would be *regrettable*—"

"But of no real importance. I understand."

"Alaric, forgive me, but Reynard doesn't *need* to attack us. You're the last living member of the royal house of Westria, and you have no heir. As your first cousin, Reynard is quite legitimately the next in line for the throne. It would be so much easier, and less costly—and certainly it would *look* much better to the world at large—if he just . . . I mean, if he and the king of Cortova really are in collusion, and you've been drawn away from the safety of your castle . . . Do you think he might . . . ?"

"Arrange an accident?"

"Something like that. More or less."

Wordlessly, the king uncorked the bottle and gave her another sip. On impulse, she grabbed it and drank down the elixir—*glug, glug, glug*—then shivered, burped, and dropped the bottle onto the coverlet.

"Goodness!" said the king, impressed.

"Double your guard, Alaric. And don't trust anyone in the court of Cortova."

The king leaned back and gazed thoughtfully out

the tiny porthole, where a brisk wind was flinging sea spray up against the glass.

"How could I possibly have missed it?" he said, shaking his head in wonder. "It's so obvious now that you've said it."

"You missed it—we both did—because it fell in with our plans."

"I suppose you're right."

He got to his feet and dragged the chair back over to the corner. There he stood for a moment, thinking his private thoughts. Molly had shut her eyes again. The talking had worn her out.

"Once we land," he said, "we'll stay on at the inn for as long as you need to recover. After that it's an easy three-day ride to the summer palace."

"Mmm," she said, already drifting back to sleep.

He continued to stand there, his hand resting on the back of the chair, searching for the words that ought to be said: how deeply indebted he was to her; how much he relied upon her wisdom, her courage, and the magical gift that led her.

And then—oh, for heaven's sake! *Relied upon? Indebted?* Those were words he might use when speaking to Mayhew or Lord Brochton. They didn't even begin to express what he owed to Molly, or what he felt, or what he feared, or the terrible sadness that crept over him as they moved inexorably toward the thing he would have to do—because he was king now, and the welfare of Westria must be his paramount concern.

From the bed he heard a soft little snore. Molly had slipped from her upright position and was tilted toward the bulkhead, her head resting against the wall, her hair in her face, and her mouth open. For some reason, seeing her like that made Alaric want to weep.

So he just said, "Thank you," very softly, and left it at that.

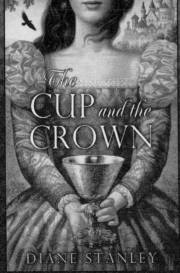